PRAISE FOR HANNAH JAYNE

"What a ride! Full of twists and turns—including an ending you won't see coming!"

—April Henry, *New York Times* bestselling author of *The Girl Who Was Supposed to Die* on *Truly, Madly, Deadly*

"Teens who enjoy R. L. Stine and Christopher Pike are the likely audience for this gripping mystery."

—*School Library Journal* on *Truly, Madly, Deadly*

"This suspenseful thriller is well paced with carefully developed characters and sharp dialogue."

—*School Library Journal* on *See Jane Run*

"Well-rounded characters spark with life in this chiller."

—*Booklist* on *The Dare*

"Brynna's guilt-induced psychosis makes for a page-turner in the spirit of Lois Duncan's classic *I Know What You Did Last Summer*; it will undoubtedly please the thriller-loving crowd."

—*Kirkus Reviews* on *The Dare*

"This mystery is marked by gripping psychological suspense and the plot builds to a dramatic conclusion."

—*Booklist* on *The Escape*

"Reminiscent of a young adult version of *Gone Girl*, *The Revenge* is a psychological thriller that hooks readers from the first page."

—*VOYA* on *The Revenge*

"Jayne crafts two perfectly imperfect protagonists and one of the most chilling psychological villains of the year… A must-read for anyone who loves thrilling crime novels."

—*School Library Journal* on *The Revenge*

ALSO BY HANNAH JAYNE

Truly, Madly, Deeply
See Jane Run
The Dare
The Escape
Twisted
The Revenge

COPYCAT

HANNAH JAYNE

sourcebooks
fire

Published by Sourcebooks Fire, an imprint of Sourcebooks, Inc.
P.O. Box 4410, Naperville, Illinois 60567-4410
(630) 961-3900
Fax: (630) 961-2168
sourcebooks.com

Library of Congress Cataloging-in-Publication Data

Names: Jayne, Hannah, author.
Title: Copycat / Hannah Jayne.
Description: Naperville, Illinois : Sourcebooks Fire, [2018] | Summary: Addie
    is obsessed with a series of mystery novels, even writing fan fiction
    based on them, but when a similar murder happens in her own town, she is
    not prepared.
Identifiers: LCCN 2017061765
Subjects: | CYAC: Mystery and detective stories. | Murder--Fiction. | Books
    and reading--Fiction. | High schools--Fiction. | Schools--Fiction.
Classification: LCC PZ7.J348 Cop 2018 | DDC [Fic]--dc23 LC record available at
    https://lccn.loc.gov/2017061765

Printed and bound in the United States of America.
VP 10 9 8 7 6 5 4 3 2 1

ONE

There was something inordinately creepy about being at school after dark. The place was deserted—the benches and picnic tables in the quad looked ominous and foreboding under the flickering yellow lights. Crystal Lanier shivered and pulled her jacket tighter against an imaginary chill. The weather was mild at Gap Lake in September; the days still sunbaked, the nights, like this one, a gentle mix of fading summer and impending fall. But the bare bones of the deserted campus had put a chill in the air, and shot a blast of cold right through Crystal.

"I'm creeping myself out," she muttered shifting her books from one arm to the other.

A wisp of wind cut through the quad. Crystal was almost sure she heard someone laughing—a weak, choked giggle, like someone was trying to swallow it down.

"Hello?"

She spun, her long black hair fanning over her shoulders. "Is someone there?" She knew she sounded like every horror movie victim ever, and her heart hammered in her throat as her skin prickled with beads of sweat.

This was Gap Lake, she reminded herself. It was a tiny town where everyone knew everyone else, and nothing bad ever happened. She was thinking that when the shadow approached. When he reached out for her long black hair. She was thinking what a nice, safe place Gap Lake was when he clamped a hand over her mouth. When he strangled her scream and drove the needle straight into her throat.

* * *

"Addison!"

Addison glanced up and blinked, feeling redness stain her cheeks and ears. She closed the book slowly, looking around at the two dozen sets of eyes staring back at her.

"I'm sorry."

Mrs. Lea took two steps forward and held out her hand. Addison cleared her throat and shifted in her seat.

"The book, Addison."

Reluctantly, Addison handed over the dog-eared book.

"Can I get it back after class, please?" she asked, her voice meek.

* * *

Maya Garcia hiked her backpack over her shoulders and stepped into the junior hallway. "Okay, how many times has Mrs. Lea taken that thing from you?"

Addison shrugged, falling into step with her best friend. "Let's see, I've read it about fifty-seven times so…fifty-six?"

"You are the biggest, nerdiest R. J. Rosen fan ever."

"Hey, I'm president of his fan club. It's mainly research."

Maya shook her head sadly. "It's borderline obsessive."

"Who you calling borderline?" Addison flashed a wide grin. "It's not entirely my fault. Rosen needs to write faster. If he could keep up with the public's rabid love for the Gap Lake mysteries, I wouldn't need to constantly reread—"

"And reread and reread. And write massive amounts of fan fiction." Addison rolled her eyes.

"Don't get me wrong, Adds. I love the books too, but you're a teenager. You need a more destructive hobby to fit in."

Addison nodded sagely. "I see where you're coming from. What do you suggest?"

"Drinking, drugs, reckless driving."

"First of all, to drive recklessly, I'd have to drive, which I will not. And as for the other stuff, what am I? A stereotype?"

Maya narrowed her eyes, crossed her arms in front of her chest. "I feel like you're not taking me seriously."

Addison stopped at locker 221 and spun the lock, pulling open the metal door. "I like to read. So what?"

Maya yanked a handful of books out of Addison's locker before dumping them back in again. "So, you should shelve a few hundred of these books and live in the here and now with the rest of us who have boyfriends who don't live only on paper."

"Number one, have you read the first Gap Lake book? Not only is Crystal's boyfriend, Declan Levy, not a one-dimensional paper product, he may or may not be responsible for her murder—I vote not. But if that doesn't make a rounded character, I don't know what does."

"Character," Maya enunciated. "That's the magic word. A character is not a real person."

"And speaking of not real people, who's this boyfriend of yours you seem to be referring to?"

A fierce blush crept across Maya's olive cheeks. "I didn't say that I had a boyfriend. But there are possibilities. Men in the wings. Plans afoot and so forth and…stuff."

"'Plans afoot'? 'So forth and stuff'? Who are you?"

Maya put her hands on her hips. "I'm your best friend, Addie. Remember me? I'm not a mystery novel, but I'm pretty damn fantastic if I say so myself."

Addie pulled the book back. She gave it a quick kiss, before stashing the book in her backpack.

Maya gaped. "Did you just kiss a book? Seriously?"

"It's my lifeblood."

Maya cocked an eyebrow and Addie shrugged.

"Okay, so it's research."

"Tell me you still want to be a writer and haven't decided on serial killing as a career goal."

"According to my father, the latter pays better."

"How is the wolf of Wall Street?"

Addie blew out a sigh. "Buying low, selling high, still wishing his disappointing daughter had a penis or a power tie."

"Well, I know what to get you for Christmas." Maya stopped dead in her tracks. "Don't look, but you're being ogled. Possibly even being fantasized about in weird and uber-sexual ways."

Addie immediately crossed her arms in front of her chest. "Now I feel skeevy."

"I'd pay a thousand bucks if Spencer Cohen was staring at me that way."

Addie shrugged, trying to play it off like she didn't care. "You need a life."

Maya groaned and shook Addie's arm. "And you need two feet in reality or you're going to prom with a cardboard cutout."

"If it's a cardboard cutout of Declan Levy, sign me up."

"So you *are* into serial killers."

"Declan didn't do it!"

Maya rolled her eyes. "Declan totally did it. He killed Crystal, then did Andy and Rhodes. It's textbook. I know because I am the daughter of cops, times two." She held up two fingers a half inch from Addie's nose. "He had motive, opportunity—all those other *CSI* words."

"That's what the author *wants* you to think. And you totally fell for it! You are so R. J. Rosen's target audience!"

"And you're his secret side chick."

Addie snorted. "I prefer biggest fan."

"Well, it seems like Spencer Cohen is your biggest fan, and he's coming over here."

"Hey, Addie." Spencer grinned, one of those three-point grins that hit his dark-brown eyes, chin dimple, and Crest-white smile.

I'm not in love with Spencer, she told herself. *Infatuation. Puppy love, maybe. He's just so cute…*

"Hey, Spencer."

Maya stepped forward. "Addie was just telling me how much she loves water polo. And dancing."

Addie blinked. "I was?"

"I play water polo." Spencer brightened and Addie gritted her teeth. She had been to nearly every one of his matches. True, she was usually up on the last bleacher with her nose in a book, but she watched whenever Spencer was in the pool. He never even noticed her.

"Yeah," she said with a slow nod. "I've seen. I mean I know. I know because I've seen you. Not in a weird way, like in a fan way. Not, like, a weird mega fan or anything but, like, a Hornets fan. You know." Addie fisted her hand and punched at the air. "Go team!"

Maya threaded her arm though Addie's and gave it a yank. "We have to go."

"Why did you do that?" Addie hissed once they were out of earshot. "Spencer and I were having a conversation."

"Have you ever heard the term *dead in the water*? Because that's what you were. 'Go team'?" She shook her head sadly.

"Did I sound that bad?"

"Yes, yes you did."

Addie sighed. "See? That's why I should stick to guys on paper."

"Oh honey," Maya slid an arm over Addie's shoulders. "At this point I don't even think your book boyfriend would talk to you."

TWO

Addie fired up her laptop, shivering when her blog, GapLakeLove, populated the screen. The new layout thrilled her. She had started with a general template two years ago—something free from the host site with cartoon flowers and streaks of black and red. Her first post was a mid-book review of R. J. Rosen's first Gap Lake book. She gushed for two pages, teasing her imaginary readers with her theories and *CSI*-style sleuthing. She pointed out foreshadowing and niggled around red herrings and murder motives. She dashed off two-hundred-word blocks of scenes she wished had been included or conversations she thought characters might have had behind closed doors. As she read the book, she went back to the site every night for three weeks, adding her own details, her own narratives, until she noticed the little page counter at the bottom of her screen: *22*. Twenty-two people had read her ramblings or landed on her site by mistake or clicked through.

No big deal.

And then the counter hit 31, 66, 74, 108…

By the time Addie was on to the next book, the counter had edged past the high four digits. The comments were trickling in: two a day, four a day—then nine for every post, eleven, eighteen, sixty-six.

She had a following.

Once her following passed twenty-six thousand, Addie invested a few bucks into the blog. She bought a premium template that she updated with an ominous, shimmering black lake overlaid with streaks of moonlight that illuminated every Gap Lake title. She had badges and awards for Best Bookish Blog, Best R. J. Rosen Readership, and Best Mystery Reader Blog. She participated in blog hops and swaps that kept fans coming and commenting. Her fans were from every corner of the world, and sometimes a publisher would contact her for a review or an interview. She was always thrilled, but the backbone of her blog was R. J. Rosen—and he was a hard fish to catch.

Fans adored Rosen's mysteries, but a big part of the mystique was R. J. Rosen himself. He was notoriously skittish, an author who shunned social media in almost all its forms. His profile photos were grainy and mysterious, obvious enough to reveal an actual person but little else. Addie felt a kinship with the reclusive genius: she was happy enough to court her fans and post on her site, but she kept her identity under wraps as much as possible. She listed herself only as blogger Lady A. Her own profile photo was shot from the back, with a swarm of her auburn hair knotted by the wind, and a swath of fog obscuring anything notable in the photo.

Mysterious—like R. J.

Even though she posted her fan fiction in the school paper, it appeared under the byline of "Lady A." For all Hawthorne students knew, the articles were pulled directly from the blog. She liked the secrecy—no matter how thinly veiled.

The new site had gone live less than two weeks ago, but there was already an arm's-length ribbon of gushing comments:

> DECLAN4EVA: I love this site so much, I feel like I'm *in* Gap Lake!
> HEARTSNSTARS: If I could 'ship myself with a blog it would be this one.
> HUBYMEGA: I want to live on this page!

The only things garnering more praise than the site's layout were R. J. Rosen's books—I've read Gap Lake: Lady of the Lake no less than eleven times and I still scream every time! and Addie's fan fiction: Are you R. J. Rosen in disguise? Either you're a great writer or a scary person in real life!

Since GapLakeLove's inception, the blog had morphed into the preeminent site for all things Gap Lake—fan fiction, theories, and whatever scraps of information she could gather from R. J. Rosen's interviews and cryptic tweets. She had been trying for four months to get Rosen on the site, which was why she let out a little yip when she saw an email in her inbox from TheRealRJRosen.

> Dear Addie,
> My publisher turned me on to your fan fiction and your site. I have to say, I'm really impressed and a little jealous! You're quite the writer, and your idea

to make Luxe "responsible" for Crystal's disappearance? Genius. Something I wish I'd thought of.

Exhilaration rushed through Addie, her cheeks aching from the press of her smile.

R. J. Rosen read her work. R. J. Rosen *liked* her work. A real published author was writing to her…was praising *her*. Her heart thundered in her chest.

Addie sat back and forced herself to breathe. The message came from someone calling himself TheRealRJRosen. How hard was it to grab a screen name?

"Probably Maya," she said with an annoyed huff.

But she kept reading.

As you know I'm currently working on the last book in the Gap Lake series. We've been working on some launch ideas to make it really special, and one thing that I would like to do is reach out to some of my biggest fans—those who, like you, have been particularly loyal to me and the crew of Gap Lake. Would you be interested in helping out with some promotional opportunities?

If the email came from Maya, it would have ended with something like "get a real boyfriend" or "call your amazing best friend."

This was a legitimate email.

R. J. Rosen, the author, was emailing *her*. He was asking *her* to be a part of his team. Butterflies went crazy in Addie's stomach and she started to tear up, swelling with pride.

Her dream could come true.

She was being asked to work with one of the hottest authors on the planet.

Addie's fingers flew over the keyboard. She wrote, read, and rewrote her response to Rosen four times before hitting Send.

She grabbed her cell phone.

"Omigod, omigod, omigod!"

"You can just call me Maya, Adds. And hello to you too."

"Guess who just contacted me? Oh my God, I'm totally shaking. Totally. Shaking. I can't—I can't—"

"Okay, okay, I'm dying here!"

"R. J. Rosen!"

There was a long pause on Maya's end of the phone.

"Did you hear me? Maya, did you hear what I said? R. J. Rosen just emailed me. R. J. Rosen, author of the Gap Lake series. My favorite author ever! Just emailed me. Asking for me to help with promotional opportunities for the book. Can you believe it?"

"Okay," Maya paused, sucking in a long, slow breath before beginning again. "I'm not saying this to be mean. Because you're my best friend and because we had that antibullying assembly last week. But why would R. J. Rosen, who's like a huge, huge megastar, write to, like, kind of a huge nobody? And I mean that in the nicest way possible."

Addie's eyebrows rose. "Wow, remind me to nominate you for best friend of the year award. Anyway, I might be kind of a nobody to you, but I'm pretty well known in the Gap Lake community."

"You write fan fiction and have, like, seven followers."

"My fan fiction is published in the school paper!"

"Right, sorry. So you have negative seven followers."

"Yeah, well, I have *twenty-seven thousand* followers online. Either way, R. J. Rosen wrote to me and asked if I wanted to do some promotional stuff for the new Gap Lake book. And if you were really my best friend, you would see how totally awesome and amazing this is for me."

"R. J. Rosen, or R. J. Rosen's publicity team?"

"R. J. Rosen. R. J. Rosen himself," Addie said.

"I don't buy it. Forgive me, but I'm the daughter of cops, remember? Don't you think it's the least bit weird that an author would be writing to bloggers? Like, I don't know what authors do all day—I'm assuming it's make up shit and eat bonbons. But I really doubt they spend their days trolling blog sites and writing to teenagers. Not that you're not super totes amazeballs, of course."

"Okay, okay. In any other instance I would totally agree with you. Like, if Stephen King dropped me a note and was all 'hey, what's up, let's be friends.' But R. J. Rosen is different. He started out self-publishing and only crossed over to a major publisher when his books went mega gangbusters and he couldn't keep up with fan demand. But he kept total creative control and is super anti-establishment. I don't even know if he has a publicist."

"My gerbil has a publicist."

Addie grinned. "That's right. How is Sir Fuzzy Pants McGinnis?"

"Ask his publicist."

"Aren't you at least a little bit happy for me?"

"I'm sorry, Addie." Maya's voice rose a little, her excitement mounting. "You're right. This actually is pretty cool. So you're going to do it, right?"

Addie bounded up, and began to pace her bedroom. "Of course I am. I mean, I don't even know what 'it' is. Oh my gosh, what if he wants to meet me?"

"What if he wants you to go on a book tour with him?"

Addie stopped. "Does that even happen?"

"I don't know, but if it does I want to be your roadie. Like, I'll lift all the books or turn all your pages or something."

Addie cocked her head when she heard the rumble of the garage door opening one floor down. "Ugh, Dad's home."

"Time to dump GapLakeLove for the NASDAQ?"

Addie grinned. "NASDAQ? Look who is learning big financial terms!"

"Please, Adds, I know that you're this tortured writer and everything, but being the daughter of a hotshot banker-dude has its perks. Your house is huge. You got a brand-new car on your sixteenth birthday. You have a freaking credit card! You know what I have? A paper route and a ten-speed."

"First of all, our house isn't that big. And the car was kind of a twisted apology gift. I'm not getting behind the wheel of that purveyor of death, so it's nothing but a pretty paperweight as far as I'm concerned. Credit card? For emergency purposes only. And you have neither a paper route nor a ten-speed. You have a good job at a retail food establishment and semi-reliable transportation."

"I work at Hot Dog on a Stick and have a stone-age Honda

Accord. But you're good with the spin. I can see why R. J. Rosen came to you. Talk to you later, Adds."

"Later, Mys."

"Addison?" Morton Gaines poked his head through Addie's open door just as she shoved her phone into her back pocket. "Working on homework?" His hazel eyes flashed to Addie's laptop. She slammed the thing closed and smiled widely.

"Totally. Some stuff for the paper too."

The fatherly smile fell from her dad's lips. "Are you still writing that fan fiction?"

"It's a column, Dad, and tons of kids read it. It's one of the most popular things in the paper." *And on my fan site,* Addie wanted to add. But she knew better. Morton Gaines was all about what looked good, what worked well, and what made money. And writing fan fiction did none of those things.

"You know if you were to actually get on the paper staff, make it a class instead of a club activity, it would look great on your college transcripts. Every little bit helps when you want to get into Stanford." He grinned and rolled up on his toes, one of those sitcom dad moves that made Addie's stomach churn.

But I don't want to get into Stanford.

"Yeah, sure. I'll look into it."

There was an awkward pause that seemed to stretch for eons. For a moment, Addie missed her old dad, the one she had before the accident and before the trial and before he came home from work early three nights a week to attend court-mandated Alcoholics Anonymous meetings.

"Anyway"—she drummed her fingers on her laptop—"I really should get back to work. Gotta keep those grades up, right?"

Addie's father offered her a thin smile, then nodded sharply. "Louisa left dinner in the oven. Be down in ten?"

"Yeah."

* * *

The shriek of the school bell shot through the classroom and Addie's brain. She slammed her history book shut and was in the hall before most of the kids in her class had even stood up. She was pacing in front of room 32B when Maya came out.

"Finally, finally, finally! I have been waiting at least twenty minutes for you. What were you doing, hanging out with Mr. Hoover?"

Maya pursed her lips and raised an unamused eyebrow. "The bell just rang. And while I have it on good authority that no one hates school more than I do, I'm beginning to think that I have competition."

"I don't hate school. I just needed to talk to you. And you would ace all your classes if you'd just apply yourself the teensiest bit." She held her thumb and forefinger a hairbreadth apart.

Maya's upper lip quirked. "You really wanted to get me out of class to do your best impression of my parents? Awesome."

"No, it's this!" She held up her phone a half inch from Maya's face, waving and grinning.

"Oh my gosh! You have your own cell phone! Way to go, Addison! You're like every sixth grader in the country."

Addie's nostrils flared as she blew out an annoyed breath and began reading.

The room was pitch-black. Completely cavernous. It felt cold and there was a smell in there, something vague and off. Something that Jordan recognized. She wrinkled her nose. Swampy. The school auditorium smelled swampy, like mud and old pond water.

"What?" She whispered to herself. "Why would—"

She heard the drips. Slow at first, then more insistent.

"Hello?" She knew no one would answer her. But she was compelled to call out as she nudged her toe along the aisle, pressing her hands against the wall.

"There has to be a light switch around here somewhere," she muttered, still moving slowly, cautiously through the darkness. Finally, her fingertips brushed against it and she flipped the switch.

Maya put her hand on Addie's shoulder. "Did you write that? It's actually kind of good."

Addie shook her head, then kept reading.

Suddenly the auditorium, the stage, everything was ablaze with yellow light. The sound system flashed on, circus music swelling so loud it thumped in Jordan's chest.

And the smell of swamp water made sense.

A scream rose in her chest but died at her lips.

It was Luxe, onstage. She was stretched out, laid on top of a table. Her white dress was soaking wet and clung to her. Her arms were outstretched, so pale that Jordan could see them turning blue as water dripped from her clawed fingertips.

She didn't want to, but Jordan couldn't stop herself. She was compelled to move closer, to go toward Luxe's outstretched body. The swamp smell grew stronger. Jordan could see the slick green-brown of beach grass wrapped around Luxe's bare legs, at her shoulders and throat.

"Oh my God!" Maya shoved her hands against her mouth, eyes wide, before grinning. "Read the rest, read the rest!" she said, hopping from foot to foot. "How did you get this? Is this for real?"

Addie slipped her phone into her back pocket, satisfied. "I told you. It's from R. J. Rosen. There is more but… How cool is it that he wrote me back? He. Wrote. Me. Back!"

Maya's eyes lit up. "The author?" Her hands immediately went to her long hair. She smoothed it, brushing it all over one shoulder and looking around. "Is he here? Oh my God, is he here?"

"What are you doing? He's not here. Why are you doing that?"

"Uh, newscasts? We could be on TV. I mean, my best friend is, like, *best friends* with the hottest writer out there. Why is this not being filmed?"

"Because R. J. Rosen just sent me an email." She shot Maya a smirk, rolling a strand of her shoulder-length hair around her fingers. "And a chunk of his story…"

Maya frowned. "That's it? Oh."

"Thanks for the support. Look, I have very little in my life. You should be excited. Listen to this:

"I'm so glad you've decided to participate in the launch activities! While I can't give you explicit details just yet, I can tell you that there will be a number of exciting stunts leading up to the book's debut. And because you have proven to be such an asset to me and the team launching

Gap Lake, you will be privy to some inside information about the story, the new book, and the characters. You'll be posting new stories—this one included—right on your own blog. Use the hashtag #GapLakeFinale to get fans wanting more!"

Maya gave a half shrug. "Well that's pretty interesting, I guess. I mean, vague but cool, right?"

"Yes, but the story!"

"Yeah, it's good. What are you supposed to do with it though?"

Addie held up her phone, and made a big show of hitting a button. "This."

Maya blinked. "That. Was. Neat?"

"I just posted the story. To my site. So all my fans are going to read it and freak, and R. J. Rosen is going to drive even more traffic to my site. Get it?"

"Not really. But if it makes you happy, then I'm happy."

Addie smiled. "That's all I ask."

"Ride home?"

Addie didn't take her eyes off her phone. "No thanks. Staying late to work on the paper."

Maya pushed out her lower lip. "Boo. I was hoping to hang poolside at your place. Maybe have your maid bring us some umbrella drinks."

Addie glanced back at her phone. "I already have fifty-four hits. There are fifty-four hits and I posted one minute ago! Listen: 'you're creepy!' 'OMG, scared to death!' Also, the woman who made umbrella drinks is gone. We've got Louisa now."

"I liked umbrella drink maid! What happened to her?"

Addie shrugged. "Pretty sure it was the fact that she offered her boss's daughter an umbrella drink."

"You ruin everything. And how are people even posting comments? How fast do people read in the blogosphere?" Maya grabbed Addie's phone, a wide, goofy smile moving across her lips. "Dude, Addie, you're famous. People are constantly hitting this thing!"

"It's kind of cool, right?"

"I take back everything I said. It's super cool. You're going to be, like, the female Stephen King. The girl guru of all things horror!"

Addie took her phone back, unable to hide her own beaming grin. "Yeah. Don't mess with me, or I'll put you in a book and kill you!"

* * *

"Okay, I'm taking pizza orders for tonight." Colton Hayes held up his cell phone, finger hovering over the Notes app. "Tell Big Daddy what you want."

Maya spun, her eyes like daggers. "Jesus, Colton! How do you always sneak up on people? You're like a thousand feet tall! Someone should put a damn bell on you."

Colton blushed beet red and Addie hid a smile. She knew she should feel sorry for the guy—his sole desire in life was to be noticed by Maya for something other than being enormous and silent. But he had the annoying tendency of showing up in the middle of conversations and referring to himself as "Big Daddy."

"Hey, Colton," Addie said. She had a soft spot for him. Not only did he have an incredible mind for all things web and editorial, he was the editor at large of the school paper and Addie's next-door neighbor.

"You guys are staying to finish laying out the paper tonight, right?"

Addie nodded. "Yeah, of course. I'm part of the team!"

Maya rolled her eyes. "I'm not, but could I get in on that pizza?"

Addie pinched her mooch of a best friend, but Colton was too deeply in love to care. He nodded vigorously and held up his phone. "What do you want me to order for you?"

THREE

"I hate being at school when it's dark. It's so unnatural." Maya shuddered.

Addie balanced her laptop on her hip as she reached for the door to the journalism room. "And yet you're here when you don't need to be."

"I needed to have free pizza."

"I thought you worked tonight."

"And I thought you understood that woman cannot live on Hot Dog on a Stick alone. I'm going to work after this. Why is the building so dark? Aren't Colton and his lackeys supposed to be here already?"

"Colton went to get the pizza and I'm the lackey."

Maya grinned. "So it's just going to be you and Colton tonight once I take my pizza and bail? Hot."

"Yes. Me, Colton, Kelly Weiss, Lydia Stevenson, Mr. Moreau."

"That sounds like a disgusting orgy. Do me a favor and don't take any pictures."

Addie stopped walking when her phone pinged.

"Oh my gosh!" She grinned.

"You say that a lot."

"Get used to it. R. J. Rosen sent me a new message. The subject line is 'Get Ready for a Surprise.'" She let out a little squeal. "He's so awesome! I bet it's the rest of the chapter he sent earlier."

Maya groaned. "That's not awesome. Unless it's directly followed by his credit card number."

Addie shook her head and tucked her phone in her back pocket. She pulled open the door to the journalism room, felt along the wall for a light switch. "I guess we're the first ones here."

"Aren't there supposed to be safety lights in here or something?"

Addie shrugged. "It's weird that Mr. Moreau isn't here yet."

"It smells weird. Does it always smell so weird in here?"

"You're so dramatic. Here's the—" Addie flicked the switch and the lights blazed bright. "Oh my God! Lydia, you scared the hell out of me."

All of the desks in the journalism room were pushed against the walls, save for one. It was set in the middle of the room and occupied by Lydia Stevenson, Hawthorne High's It Girl, head cheerleader, and lead journalist. She was facing forward, with her back toward Maya and Addie, and her head on the desk.

"Lydia? Why were you sitting in the dark?"

Maya sniffed at the air. "It smells like dirt. Why does it—" Maya took a step closer to Lydia, to the single desk, and stopped. "Lydia? Are you okay? You're…"

Lydia had her head on the desk. Her long blond hair was fanning down in a graceful wave, but it was stained a deep brown.

Mud colored.

Like her bare feet.

"Addie?"

Addie was closing in on Lydia too, slowly, carefully.

"Don't say it, Maya."

Maya reached out a shaking hand, her fingertips brushing over Lydia's bare arms. They were cold. Ice cold.

"She…she's dead. I think she's dead."

Addie's phone pinged a second time. Stomach churning, she glanced at the readout, a sob dying in her chest.

TheRealRJRosen:

Did you like my surprise?

FOUR

It was like all the oxygen had been sucked out of the room. Addie started to shake, a violent tremor that started low in her gut and rocked through her until her teeth were chattering.

"No," she finally managed. "No."

"Addie, she's—"

In her mind, Addie was shaking her head. In her mind, she was shaking her head and touching Lydia's shoulder, and Lydia was waking up and this was all a really bad dream.

"We have to call the police. Call 911."

Maya was talking, making sense, but Addie couldn't force herself to move. Finally, in molasses-like slow motion, she willed her arm to move. Her hand to grab her phone. She held her phone up, ready to dial, when the message from R. J. Rosen blazed again.

"Did you like my surprise?"

"Addie, dial. Do you hear me? Dial your phone!"

Addie forced her mouth to move. "R. J.—"

Maya stamped her foot and grabbed Addie by the shoulders,

spinning her to face forward. "Stop with the R. J. Rosen stuff! You need to call the police! Lydia is—"

"Please don't say it."

Maya snatched the phone from Addie's hand and dialed, pacing while Addie stayed still, rooted to the floor. She didn't want to look at Lydia, but her eyes would go nowhere else.

She's not dead, she reasoned. *Maya doesn't know.*

She's sleeping.

Yes, Addie told herself, Lydia is sleeping. Passed out, maybe.

But the message R. J. Rosen sent…

Addie could hear Maya's disembodied voice. She knew she was right behind her, but Maya sounded like she was a million miles away, her voice shaking as she spoke. "Mom? It's me. There's… we're at school and…"

Addie put her hands over her head, pressing his palms to her ears. She didn't want to hear it. She didn't want to hear Maya talking to her mother, the chief of police. She didn't want to hear that they were in the journalism room with a dead body.

Lydia Stevenson was a dead body.

No.

That can't be right.

Addie had seen Lydia at lunch today. She was sitting with Spencer Cohen; they had broken up, but she was still fawning over him. And now Lydia was dead.

"The police are on their way." Maya stretched an arm across Addie's shoulders. "Come on, let's wait outside."

Addie forced her lips to move. "We shouldn't leave her."

Maya shuddered, her voice finally starting to crack. "I don't want to stay in here with…" Addie could tell that Maya didn't want to look at Lydia, what was left of her, hunched and crumpled over her desk. "I can't stay in here."

* * *

It didn't take long for the police to arrive, their cruisers screaming through the cold night air. But Colton arrived first, the smell of hot, greasy pizza hitting Addie before Colton hit the first step. She doubled over and dry heaved.

"Uh, sorry. Did you not want pepperoni?" His grin was wide and lopsided, dropping from his face when the first siren blared. "You called the cops? I paid for the pizza out of petty cash. Mr. Moreau said I could."

"No." Addie's voice was a choked whisper.

"What's going on?"

"It's…it's…" Maya looked helplessly from Colton back over her shoulder through the glass doors to where Lydia was. "It's Lydia. We think she's—"

Again, Addie willed Maya not to say it. Not to say that Lydia was dead, because if she did, it would be out there and it could be true.

People her age didn't die.

Teenagers *she knew* didn't die. People in the past did. Photographed faces of people she never met from old Hawthorne yearbooks died. Those people died, while Addie's life in the here and now and the lives of her friends and family plowed on day after day, Monday after Monday, because that was life and that was what Addie knew.

She didn't know this. Sure, she read about death in her books. Gap Lake was filled with death: murder, mayhem, undercover abuse from seemingly perfect families. But this was real life. And in real life, red, white, and blue police lights were cutting through the night, splashing across the faces of Addie's friends. Maya, her cheeks tearstained and red. Colton, pizza still in his hands, dark eyes drawn and wild-looking as he glanced from the approaching cars to Maya and Addie.

"You guys, what's happening?"

The first officer was in the parking lot. His squad car was parked in the student drop-off and Addie had the ridiculous thought that she should tell him he couldn't stop there. Then another squad car and another, until uniformed police were swarming the school. One approached Addie, Maya, and Colton.

"Which one of you found the victim?"

"Lydia," Addie heard someone say. "Her name is Lydia." It took her a half second to realize that she was the one talking, her voice sounding cool and even in the night air. "We found her. But she's just…" She let her words trail off and a second officer, this one a woman with close-cropped blond hair and a name badge that said Olson, offered Addie a smile that was somewhere between authoritative and apologetic.

"Why don't you come with me and we can talk?"

Addie pumped her head, then knitted her fingers, pressing her palms together so hard they hurt. She didn't know what to do with her hands. What do people being questioned by the police do with their hands? She gulped, then cleared her throat, shifting her weight from foot to foot.

"Where's Mr.—" Maya stopped talking.

"Mr. Moreau," Addie answered.

The journalism teacher pulled into the parking lot, his bald head on swivel as lights from the squad car flashed across his windshield, illuminating his anemic lips that were pulled into a thin line. As the officers approached him in a tight bunch, he held up his hands, palms facing forward.

"Oh my God," Addie murmured. "Oh my God, do you think he did it?"

Nobody answered and the swarm of noises—shouting, the yip of the sirens, the general buzz of radio chatter and static—swarmed around Addie, a thrum that pulsed through her and tickled the backs of her ears.

"What's going on here?" Mr. Moreau's usually calm voice was pinched and tight as he exited his car. "Are my students—is everything okay?"

"Addison?" It was Officer Olson again. Addie could feel a warm weight on her arm. She blinked at the hand that was there: rounded nails clipped short and glossy, a wedding ring. A watch with fat digital numbers flashed in a hazy blue.

"Is Mr. Moreau in trouble?" she heard herself ask.

"We're just going to talk to him, just like I'd like to talk to you, okay?"

The woman smiled. Addie tried to nod but could only focus on the weight of the hand on her arm.

"Please, can someone just tell me what is going on here?" She heard Mr. Moreau's voice through the din. "Addison? Colton? Are you guys okay?"

Addie lifted her hand and waved, an odd little finger wave that felt like betrayal. Lydia was dead and she was waving. Her breath caught in her throat and her eyes started to water.

"Try and calm down," Officer Olson told her. "Why don't you take a few deep breaths?"

Addie, generally a devout rule follower, tried to do as she was told. She tried to smile but it felt like she was grimacing, her bared teeth cold against the night air. She cleared her throat, tried to suck in a deep breath—*how does one breathe again?*—then clamped her eyes shut.

After a second, she took out her phone to call her dad, but before she could, she noticed a new message. She opened it, and R. J. Rosen's words flooded in front of her.

…Luxe looked like she was sleeping. She was on her side on the table, her hip and shoulder lined up perfectly, her knees crooking across the faux wood grain. Her arm was curled under her head. Jordan remembered thinking she looked peaceful, and that was how her friend always looked when she spent the night and slept in, one leg splaying out of her sleeping bag, her dark hair fanned out behind her. But when she looked closer, she knew her friend wasn't sleeping. Her body was too still, too perfect, too crooked. Her fingers weren't splayed, they were clawed—and her fingernails…Jordan narrowed her eyes and her breath caught in her throat. First from that deathly, muddy, swampy smell, and second from the sight of Luxe's nails: filthy, her cuticles caked with dirt and brick-red blood. Her manicure was broken, the paint—no, Jordan realized with a sickening feeling, the nail was peeling back and splintered. She doubled over and retched, coughing

29

and gasping and clawing at her throat. Her friend was dead. She was at school, where Crystal and Luxe and she had been, it seemed, almost every day of their friendship and their lives, and here she was alive and desperate to breathe but her friend would never breathe again...

"R. J. Rosen," Addie whispered.

"What's that?" the police officer said.

"I was reading..."

Maya looked up and pinned Addie with a low-eyebrowed glare. "Addie, stop," she hissed.

The officer looked from Addie to Maya, then pulled a tiny leather notebook from her enormous tool belt and produced a pen. "Can we start over?"

Addie blinked, her eyes dry but a mammoth lump forming in her throat.

"My name is Officer Christina Olson. What's your name?" She was looking directly at Addie. Addie's mind reeled, but she knew the answer to this question.

"My name is Addie. Addison Gaines."

The officer cocked her head. "Gaines, like Morton Gaines?"

"Like Morton Gaines Investments," Maya said under her breath.

Even with thousands of devoted blog followers, Addie wasn't famous—but her father was. He was Morton Gaines, investment banker extraordinaire, and if you had money, he was your best friend. If you had money, he attended your wedding and bought your children birthday gifts and made your small fortune into a big one. If you didn't have money or were his only daughter, you barely existed.

Addie cleared her throat. "Yeah, that's my dad."

"Hmm," Officer Olson scribbled something on her notepad. Addie shifted her weight. She waited for the inevitable, for the officer to ask her about that event—about that case.

But that was a lifetime ago and tonight, at her own high school, a girl was dead.

"Hello, Maya," Officer Olsen said.

Maya nodded to the officer. Both her parents were police officers—her mother, chief of police; her father, a homicide detective, which gave her some amazing street cred but meant she couldn't walk in a circle without the entire police force knowing where she was.

"You mentioned another name a second ago. R. J.—something?"

"R. J. Rosen. He's—"

Maya's eye roll was almost audible. "R. J. Rosen is an author. He writes those Gap Lake books. Addie's a mega fan. I don't know why she keeps bringing him up."

Officer Olson smiled. "Right, Gap Lake. I've read one or two of those. My niece loves those things. Pretty good, but I have to say there's a lot of shoddy police work in them." She smiled and Addie immediately warmed to her. Maya grimaced.

"You realize a girl is dead, right?" Her voice was soft and even, dripping with contempt.

"Wait, no one said…no one said…" Colton was taking baby steps backward, holding up his big hands, palms forward. All the color had drained from his face. "It's Lydia? Are you…are you sure?"

"Yes," Maya supplied. "Lydia, in the journalism room."

Addie had the horrible urge to giggle. Maya sounded like she was about to win a round of Clue.

"Why did you bring up R. J. Rosen, Addie?"

Addie looked at the message on her phone, suddenly overcome with how silly she was about to sound. Finally, she shrugged. "I don't know. It just, it felt like a book." Her voice went up at the end, like she was asking a question. "I thought maybe..." She looked at her sneakers, then kicked at the cement in front of her. "I don't know."

FIVE

"Hello?"

Addie wasn't exactly expecting anyone to answer. It was after eight and although half the lights in the house were blazing, she knew her father wouldn't be home yet. She dumped her backpack in the hallway, knowing that she should pick it up but couldn't be bothered to. Everything ached. Her eyes were dry from a combination of crying over Lydia and staring wide-eyed, as the police asked her again and again what happened.

"I walked in the room," she had replied. "I smelled something wet, swampy-like."

Swampy.

That was the same word that R. J. Rosen had used, wasn't it? "Jordan smelled something muddy, swampy…"

Addie shook it off. R. J. Rosen was a good writer. He did research. He wrote about real-life events, and, in real life, teens died.

A shiver walked up Addie's spine and she tried to rub the chill from her skin.

Teens weren't supposed to die.

She walked through the enormous foyer and snapped on every light until the room glowed, soft white light bouncing off the ridiculous marble floors, the ugly vase that was worth a fortune.

Addie hated this house.

She had been seven when they had moved in. And she had loved it. It was a fairly new development, but now, almost all the houses were occupied. She used to ride her bike through the red mud and the new construction, revel in the fact that her bedroom was the size of a small apartment with its own bathroom and a bathtub fit for a mermaid. It was way too big for just Addie and her father, but she hadn't realized that yet and loved every nook and hiding spot, loved roaming the neighborhood. She was too young then to realize the house was a stupid status symbol of something they didn't really have. It wasn't a home. But then again, she and her dad weren't really a family.

Louisa, the latest woman who helped out around the house, had left her a plate in the microwave, covered with cling film and loaded with goopy-looking vegetables and something baked with potatoes.

Addie threw it in the trash.

Her stomach had been in knots since Officer Olson had stared her down, had turned off that kindly smile and gone "all business" on her, asking the same question four different ways until Addie was tripping over her own tongue. Addie had known that she didn't have to answer them, that she didn't have to talk to the police. That happened in every Gap Lake novel: the police came out to interview the tearful, hapless bystanders, teens who didn't have to talk if their parents weren't present. But Addie didn't want to seem guilty, so she told her story again and again, each time they asked, until her mouth was dry and her throat ached.

Her cell phone chirped and she let out a tiny scream, clutching her chest and holding the thing to her ear. "Jesus, Maya, you scared the crap out of me."

"Sorry. I know, I'm pretty jumpy too. You alone?"

Addie hiked herself up on the counter. "What do you think?"

"Did you have to let the staff go?"

"Very funny. What's up?" She could hear Maya shifting on her end of the phone, could hear the vibration of Maya's voice. "Are you in the bathroom?"

"No. Yes. I was calling to see if you want company."

"I'm coming to your place," both girls said simultaneously.

Maya lived in a nondescript home in a tract of equally nondescript homes. Each room was a perfect square with a single square window and four walls painted eggshell and carpeted wall to wall with unobtrusive almond-colored carpet. The furniture was just as nondescript and unobtrusive, and Addie never asked but was vaguely sure the barely beige sofa set that matched the lamp shade that matched the drapes must have come with the house.

"The police are at your house. I'm coming over," Addie said.

"No, the police are at the station. My mom threatened to send Officer Hale to come 'check in on me.' So I said I'm going to your place."

"You get a police escort? That's awesome."

"No," Maya said slowly. "I'm a seventeen-year-old with a

babysitter in combat boots. I'm coming to your place. Your place is awesome. You're just blind to its awesomeness."

"It's a freaking prison," Addie said, hopping off the counter.

"With gilded bars. Whilst I am in a prison of beige. Of"—Addie imagined her best friend spinning around her bedroom, glancing at the eggshell walls, her fingers flitting over the beige curtains—"almond excrement. And you have better snacks. And a pool."

Addie sighed. "I guess I can't argue with that and your exceptional use of the word 'whilst.' Get over here."

"You think your dad would mind if I spent the night? Everyone's at work and I don't want to be alone."

Addie shrugged. "If he shows up, I'll ask him." She paused. "Are they working on Lydia's case?"

Lydia's case. It just sounded off. Someone she knew had a police case—no, Addie corrected herself. *Was* a case. Gooseflesh shot out along her arms. "Just get over here, okay?"

Addie left her cell phone to charge on the kitchen counter and went to her bedroom, stripping out of her clothes and dumping them on the floor. She glanced at the heap, briefly wondering if she should bag them, if the police would ask for them for evidence.

You're being crazy, she told herself. *All you and Maya did was find the body.*

Her heart ached.

Lydia was now "the body."

She didn't want to believe it. Couldn't believe it but couldn't get it out of her mind.

She stepped into the shower and turned the knob, getting the water as hot as she could stand. When the bathroom was waist high with steam, Addie stepped in, letting the water pour over her, pinning her skin, giving her goose bumps.

Tonight, she and her best friend had seen a dead body.

Lydia.

Slumped.

Arms folded.

What had happened to her?

She wasn't bleeding.

Overdose?

Addie didn't know Lydia as much as she knew *of* her. She was pretty, popular—didn't those two always go hand in hand?—she was friendly enough. Captain of the debate team. A cheerleader. A fairly good student. But drugs?

Addie thought back to the first time she had seen Lydia in her element. It was at a party at Brian Briggs's house and Addie and Maya hadn't exactly snagged an invite, but the party was big enough and loud enough that no one noticed when they slipped in. Addie, nervous, licking her newly painted Raging Red lips.

"Stop that," Maya had said, giving the flesh above Addie's arm a good pinch.

"I can't help it," Addie said, blotting her lips. "I'm nervous. We've never been to a high school party before."

"And we never will again if you keep licking your lips like that. People are going to think you have herpes."

Addie arched an eyebrow. "I really need to find better friends."

Maya grinned. "You know you love me. And you look amazing."

Addie caught a glimpse of herself in the full-length mirror in the Briggses' foyer and almost didn't recognize herself. Short skirt. Knee-high boots. Flimsy shirt that showed off a little too much cleavage. She squirmed, but Maya pinned her with a stare and brushed her hair over her shoulders. "Stop. You really look incredible. Give yourself a little credit. Spencer is going to go nuts."

A little shiver went through Addie.

She told Maya that all she'd ever wanted was Declan Levy—straight from the pages of Gap Lake. And it was true—because she didn't want to be in love with Spencer Cohen. She did her best to dismiss him and his chiseled water polo shoulders and his Mediterranean perma tan.

She read about Declan and dreamed about Declan, but she knew he wasn't real.

But Spencer was.

She didn't want her heart to speed up when he looked at her, didn't want her temperature to ratchet up ten degrees when he grinned. Every time he walked by, her body betrayed her—and she didn't hate it.

He had chestnut-colored hair. It was just shaggy enough on top that Addie could push it out of his hot-chocolate-colored eyes. She imagined him batting his long lashes at her, then dragging his tongue over his full lips…

"Addie, Addie! Earth to Addison!"

"Oh. Hi. Wait. What?"

"He's right there. Are you going to make your move?" Maya jutted her chin toward the open sliding glass door. The pool glistened in the darkness and standing there, framed in the brilliance, was Spencer. He

blinked when he saw Maya, but grinned when he saw Addie, raising the red plastic cup in his hand.

Addie melted. She smiled so hard her cheeks hurt and tried to offer a casual wave in return.

The smile dropped from Spencer's lips.

"Oh," he mouthed. "Not you. Sorry."

Addie felt the brush from the girl behind her. A whiff of jasmine-scented perfume. The swish of perfect blond locks.

"Spencer!" Lydia Stevenson stepped in front of Addie and beelined toward him, rushing into his arms. Spencer hugged her tight, but offered a crooked apologetic smile toward Addie.

She swallowed hard, feeling the heat rush through her body, burning the tops of her ears. Somewhere behind her, she heard the snickers. The whispers. Everyone saw it. Everyone saw her wave to a guy who was waving to another girl.

"Can we go?"

Rumors swelled that Lydia had gotten sloppy drunk that night and gone skinny-dipping before being carried home by Spencer. But now…

Addie shot shampoo in her hand and rubbed it into her hair, closing her eyes against the suds. But each time she did, she saw Lydia, saw her hunched over the desk, the blue-white of her skin.

Lydia was gone.

Dead.

There would only be stories, only memories.

Addie shivered even under the hot water. She turned it off and stepped into the steam-filled bathroom, wrapping herself in a

39

fluffy pink towel from the rack. The steam started to clear, leaving bubbles of condensation at the edges of the fogged-up mirror. That's when she saw it. Eye height. Crude letters finger-scrawled across the steamy mirror.

I'M HERE.

SIX

Addie's heart started to thud, and she found it hard to breathe. The steam was thick, choking, and she started to cough. She clawed for the door, but it wouldn't open.

"What? What the—oh God." She started to pound. "Help me! Help me! Dad? Dad?"

The door was snatched open from the other side and Addie went barreling to the ground, towel in a heap around her. She was panting and crying and Maya was staring down at her.

"Oh my gosh, Addie, what's wrong? What happened?"

"Someone was in the bathroom with me! I was in the shower and when I got out there was a message on the mirror!" Tears streamed down her face and she was heaving—then immediately stopped, dropping her head in her hands. "You went in the bathroom, didn't you?"

Maya bit her lip, nodded sheepishly. "I'm so sorry. I didn't mean to scare you. I wrote it."

"You wrote 'I'm here' because—" Addie rolled onto her butt on the carpet and adjusted the towel around her. "Because you're here. Oh my God, I'm so lame."

She started to giggle, and Maya sat down next to her. "You kind of are. But in your defense, we're both really freaked out. Someone was murdered, Adds. Someone we know. And we"—Maya sucked in a slow, painful breath—"found her."

Addie's eyes widened. "We don't know she was murdered. We don't know that for sure. Did your parents say something?"

Maya shook her head. "No, they won't talk too much to me about an ongoing case, especially one like this. But what else could it be? People our age don't just up and die."

"It could have been drugs. Right? An overdose or something?"

"I honestly don't know what to think."

"Every time I close my eyes..." She started to pace, her hands rubbing along her crossed arms. Addie felt the gooseflesh rise. "I mean, if someone did do this, why? And who?"

"Maybe Mr. Moreau."

Addie gaped. "The journalism teacher? No. No way."

Maya scooched over. "Here's the thing. Most people are killed by people that they know." She started ticking off each finger. "Spouse or boyfriend, sibling or parent." She eyed Addie. "Employee or teacher."

"That's not true."

"Where was Mr. Moreau when Lydia was murdered?"

"I don't know. But he drove up after we found her. Like, right after, so he was probably at—I don't know—home or something, or wherever teachers go. And if not being there makes someone a suspect, then we're all suspects. You, me, and Colton."

Maya shook her head. "Colton couldn't have done it. He's too enormous."

"That's a defense?"

"And no motive. But Mr. Moreau…"

Addie rolled her eyes. "What would his motive be?"

"Love. Greed. Sex."

Now Addie ticked off on her fingers. "Mr. Moreau got married last year, Lydia worked at The Gap, so I doubt she was rolling in cash, and sex with a teacher is so beyond gross I can't even dignify that with a response."

"Fine then. Grammar?"

"As a motive?"

Maya blew out a sigh. "I'm out of ideas."

Addie pulled on some clothes and then wound her towel around her head. The pressure felt good against her throbbing temples. "So, earlier, when I was telling you about R. J. Rosen?"

Maya rolled her eyes and flopped down on Addie's bed. "Are we seriously going to have a fangirl discussion?"

"I'm serious, just hear me out."

Maya straightened up and eyed Addie anyway. "I'm sorry. Spill."

"It's weird that right before this happened Rosen sent me a snippet of the new Gap Lake book."

"Yeah. It was pretty juicy. You said there was more. Is it as good as what you read me?"

Addie stood up, then started to pace. "Yeah, I guess." She bit her lip. "So the part that I read you…Jordan goes into the school auditorium and that's where she finds Luxe."

"Why was she at the auditorium after dark? I mean, in the first book, Crystal went missing when she was at school after hours. That's kind of dumb."

"We were at school after hours."

"Yeah, but we're real people. We were working on the school paper."

"And we found Lydia. So it's pretty realistic—"

Maya's face was grim. "Life imitates art?"

Addie's stomach roiled, bile itching at the back of her throat. "Or art imitates life." She shivered. "So Jordan went back to the school auditorium because she's in the play and she left her script behind."

She waved at the air. "There was a whole backstory. That's not the point, okay? Just listen. So Jordan is at school after dark, and she goes to get her script and she finds Luxe. Her body."

"Okay."

Addie pinched her lips. "Just listen. She walks out to the auditorium and she sees Luxe, lying on the stage."

"Okay?"

"But first she smells something swampy and muddy."

"Well, that would make sense since they live in Gap Lake."

"They don't live *in* the lake. But listen: a wet, muddy smell? A swampy smell? The heroine is at school after dark?"

Maya rearranged the pillows on Addie's bed and melted into them. "I'm getting all that. I'm not sure what I'm supposed to do. Be shocked? It's a story, Addie. It's a dead character in a series that has a history of dead characters. All the books are the same. Some young chick dies and another chick finds her."

"Do I have to spell it out for you, Maya?"

"I think I've made it pretty clear that you do."

"*We* were at school after dark. And *we* found"—here, her voice cracked—"a body. Don't you see the similarities? It smelled in the journalism room. It smelled, and I used that exact word 'swampy.'"

Maya held Addie's eye for a long beat and then shrugged. "So?"

"Don't you see? I get this passage from R. J. Rosen and right afterward, right after we walked in and found Lydia, I get a text from him that says, 'Did you like my surprise?'" Addie held out her phone, the offending text open. "Don't you see?"

"I do not."

"R. J. Rosen wrote about it and then it happened. We basically walked into the book."

"So you're telling me that R. J. Rosen is trolling us? And what, plotting the murder of teens to sell more books?"

Addie flopped down next to Maya. "When you say it like that, it does sound really dumb."

"I'm sorry, hon, but when you say it any way it sounds dumb."

"It's just so coincidental."

"It's a very vague coincidence. Like, what exactly makes the Kardashians famous vague."

"Addison! Oh my gosh, Addie! Are you okay?" Addie's father was at her bedroom door, crossing her room in two full strides. "Honey, why didn't you call me?"

"I did. I left a message on your phone."

Morton Gaines strode into the room and gathered up his daughter in his arms. Addie hugged him back, loving the familiar smell of her dad's aftershave, the way the office smell hung on his suit.

"I'm so sorry. I was in a dinner meeting with some clients from—well, it doesn't matter. Hello, Maya. I'm really glad you're here with Addie. You're a good friend."

"Thanks, Mr. Gaines."

"Did you call your parents? Are they working on the case?"

Maya half shrugged, half nodded. "My dad was working tonight anyway and my mom went in after I said I was coming here." She grabbed Addie's elbow, gave it a possessive squeeze. "I didn't think Addie should be alone out here."

Mr. Gaines dismissed Maya's comment and began pacing the room. "I just can't believe the school administration didn't call me. And the police shouldn't have been allowed to talk to you without an adult present."

"They tried to call you too, Dad. And it was fine. They just asked us questions about…her. About finding her."

"Are you okay? Both of you? Do you need anything? To talk, anything?"

Addie and Maya both shook their heads. "We're fine."

Addie licked her lips. "As fine as we can be."

Then, when Mr. Gaines left, Maya leaned in. "It's so nice how concerned your dad is."

Addie snorted. "You're kidding me, right? I left four messages on his phone. We've been home for hours. I think he's more concerned that he may have missed an opportunity to sue the police than anything else."

"Addie, you know that's not true."

Addie shot her best friend a glance.

"Your father is a money man. He would have much rather let the police department settle out of court than go through a lawsuit. Way more money that way."

"Go to bed, jerk."

SEVEN

Addie tried to sleep, but all she could see was Lydia, hunkered down over her desk. She kicked off the covers and tiptoed around Maya, grabbing a Gap Lake book and trying to read, but her mind kept crowding out the words, kept stomping out the story.

What had happened to Lydia? And what did R. J. Rosen mean— *Did you like my surprise?* The thought still gave Addie chills and shot out bat wings through her gut. He must have meant the next part of the story, but it still didn't sit well with her. She grabbed her laptop and curled into her window seat, first taking a sweeping look out the window.

There were no lights on in the houses across the street, the black windows like gaping mouths and boring eyes. She was going to pull the curtain when she saw the warm yellow glow from Colton's bedroom window next door. She watched until his curtain fluttered and he stepped into the window, reaching down to shut it. Addie could see that he had on bright-green Hawthorne High sweatpants—they were enormous and bunched at his waist. He caught her eye, then smiled, offering her a finger wave.

Addie could feel the blush in her cheeks—she had been caught staring into a boy's window! But it was Colton Hayes, and he had lived next door since freshman year. He and Addie threw the occasional pebble at each other's windows, met outside here and there to talk about Gap Lake or nothing at all. Colton picked up his phone and pointed at it.

Addie grabbed hers, answering just before the first ring went through.

"Hey," he said.

"Hey," she said, whispering so as not to wake Maya. "I think it's weird that you don't text."

Colton leaned into the window, and Addie could see the enormous, ancient phone he had pressed to his ear. "Landline. My parents have this 'lock up your cell phone' after nine o'clock thing."

Addie nodded. "That's actually kind of nice."

Colton snorted. "If you want your parents to talk to you or whatever."

"I guess."

"So…are you as freaked out as I am?"

Addie swallowed the lump that started in her throat. She could only nod, then finally force out a meek "uh-huh."

"What do you think happened to her?"

Tears were rimming Addie's eyes. "I don't know. I just…" She sucked in a breath. "I know this is going to sound crazy, but I got a message from R. J. Rosen. And—"

"Wait," she could see Colton frown from his window. "The real R. J. Rosen? Like the author?"

"Yeah."

"He contacted you? Through your blog, or did he call you or something?"

Addie sucked in a slow breath. The excitement was still there, but it was tempered by the shock of the evening. "He sent me a message through GapLakeLove, and then I responded from my email so he emailed me there." The familiar thrum of excitement rolled through her and she could almost imagine that all she had was good news. "It was kind of cool. He wants me to be a part of his launch activities for the new book."

"That's awesome, Addie! You're going to be famous."

She felt heat in her cheeks and shook her head, dark hair bobbing around her shoulders. "Maybe. I doubt it. I'm just a fan."

"A fan who probably writes better than the author."

"Nobody thinks that, Colton."

"Hey, I'm just saying. People are totally talking about your blog at school. You know who even said something? Spencer."

"Spencer Cohen?"

Colton snorted. "Right? I didn't even know he could read."

Addie tried to tamp down her excitement. "I didn't know he was even into Gap Lake."

"Yeah, apparently Lydia makes him read—" Colton's words dropped off, the implication hanging there between them. "Lydia *made* him read them, I guess…"

Gap Lake. The entire school was obsessed with it. The entire town maybe.

Obsessed enough to kill?

Addie sucked in a steadying breath, her insides feelings as though they were going to collapse in on themselves. "What happened tonight…this…it sounds like it came right from the book."

"What are you talking about?"

Addie sighed again, glancing at Maya sleeping so soundly on the bed. She was on her back, covers to her chin, snoring softly. Addie wished she could sleep like that, but her stomach was in knots, her world in pieces. "Meet me downstairs and I'll show you."

Addie pulled on a sweatshirt and walked out the front door. She didn't have to worry about an angry sibling or a parent really caring that she was walking out of her house at ten o'clock at night. It took Colton a good ten minutes to make it out of his and when he did, he was dressed in all black and moving like a cat burglar—be it an enormous, lanky, and inelegant one.

"What's with the outfit?"

"If my parents spot me, I'm dead. Well, even more dead than I already am. I'm grounded."

"Because?"

Colton shrugged, sliding in a bit of cool nonchalance. "What do you think? Please say something cool like you're pretty sure I knocked over a liquor store or got caught running an online gambling ring."

"I'm betting you either blew your entire family's data plan playing something stupid like *Pokémon Go* or your grades are bad."

Colton frowned. "It's sad how well you know me. Anyway, what are you talking about with 'it came from a book'? That's weird and ominous."

Addie worried her bottom lip, trying to decide how much to tell. "Not a book. Gap Lake."

"I don't think there's a murder like Lydia's in any of the books. Definitely not the first one."

"Not that one. Something new."

"The one that isn't out yet?"

"I told you R. J. Rosen wants me to help with the launch, right? He sent me a story. It's on my blog."

Colton nodded and broke into a huge grin. "I think that's so cool, Addie. And you really deserve it, totally."

She swallowed hard, something hard and dark in her gut. "He sent this piece of the story just before"—Addie sucked in a breath, forced herself to say it—"just before we found Lydia. Then after that, he sent another message." She thumbed through her messages, then held up the phone to Colton. He squinted in the darkness.

"Did you like my surprise?"

Addie nodded.

"That's it?"

"That doesn't freak you out? Not even a little?"

Colton took her phone, raised one shoulder. "I'm sorry, Addie, but...no. He said he was going to send you a surprise. He sent you some story and then asked if you like it."

Relief, cold and damp, exploded over Addie. She couldn't hide her smile. "Do you really think that's it?"

"They don't call me the Secret Decoder for nothing."

"Colton, nobody calls you that."

He pinched his lips. "Could maybe you start that, then? Cuz I'd love to have a cool nickname in high school."

"I'll see what I can do. So I'm just being dumb and paranoid, right?"

Addie pressed her lips together. "I know. It sounds weird now that I say it. I just thought... I don't know. I think I'm just freaked out all around."

Colton shrugged, his shoulders going to his earlobes. "I know Lydia was a big fan."

"I know she read the books."

"She did. She was a big, big fan. Like, Addie Gaines big." He smiled, his white teeth straight and almost glowing. "So I guess it would be really creepy, you know? 'Author offs his biggest fan.'"

Addie wanted to smile but everything felt wrong. Morbid. Tainted.

"Yeah, I guess that's dumb."

"Colton!" A shrill voice came from over his left shoulder and Colton's face flushed a fierce red.

"And I am so, so busted."

For as big and lanky as Colton was, he moved fast. Addie heard his big feet bounding up the porch steps, then heard the gentle click as he tried his best to silently pull the door shut behind him. Then, "I'm right here, Ma. I've been here the whole time."

Addie shoved her phone into her back pocket, laughing at Colton. He was trying to convince his mother that he hadn't been out of the house. And, Addie decided, he was right—at least when it came to R. J. Rosen. Addie was being ridiculous. She grabbed her phone as she padded up the stairs, answering his message.

AddieGaines:

The story was an awesome surprise. Thanks!

He immediately responded.

TheRealRJRosen:

There's much more fun in store for you—you just wait!

Addie wasn't sure she could take much more "fun."

EIGHT

The next morning, Maya rolled over on the bed, dug through her bags on the floor, then made a mad dash for Addie's closet. She threw open the double doors and pinched her bottom lip with one hand while flicking through clothes with the other hand.

"What am I going to wear today?"

Addie nudged Maya's bag with her big toe. "Why do you bring bags when you always wear my clothes?"

Maya turned and unzipped her bag, pulling out a mammoth makeup bag and an equally large plastic tub of gummy bears.

"Because while you have impeccable taste in clothes and a credit card with a healthy limit, you have dismal taste in makeup and a pantry full of off-brand sugary treats."

Addie crossed her arms in front of her chest. "We have Godiva chocolate."

Maya chomped the head off a red gummy bear. "What are you even saying? Anyway, you love this, this is what we do. I wear all your clothes and in return—"

"You paint me up like a three-dollar hooker." She grinned.

Maya stuck out her tongue. "You love it."

"I do. It's a nice symbiosis."

Maya pulled out a yellow top, held it against her. "Look who's flaunting her higher education."

Addie sat cross-legged on her bed, flicking on the TV and changing the channels maniacally.

"What are you looking for?"

"News."

"Fascinating."

"News about last night," Addie said. She flipped channel after channel. "There has to be something. A girl is dead. Did your parents send you any information?"

Maya thumbed through her phone. "Contrary to popular belief in this room, my parents don't send me criminal updates. But they do want me to be sure to have a healthy breakfast and not eat too much sugar." She deleted the text while an anchorwoman broke into a segment on outdoor cooking. The Super News 6 icon shot across the screen, the words *Breaking News* emblazoned in animated red underneath.

"This is it."

Maya shook her head, turning from the TV. "I don't want to watch. I was there, I know."

Addie turned the TV's volume up anyway, leaning in.

"Tragedy strikes at Hawthorne High," the buffed and coiffed reporter began. "Last night, two students from Hawthorne High School discovered the body of a third in the school journalism department. So far, there has been no confirmation on the identity of the victim or the circumstances surrounding the death. The police are saying that the death looks suspicious, but are offering no further statements. And now, on to weather."

Addie clicked off the TV and frowned. "That's it? Her name is Lydia Stevenson."

"Was," Maya said softly, eyes downcast. "Her name *was* Lydia Stevenson."

Addie tried to blink away the tears that rimmed her lower lashes, tried to shrug off the heat that crawled up her vertebrae. "That's it? That's all they're going to say? What happened to her? Don't they know yet? They had all night." She was off the bed, pacing, anger rippling through her.

Maya was shaking her head, arms crossed. "This is the way it goes, Addie. It takes time for a police investigation to go forward."

"But we know her, Maya. We know her, and we told the police exactly who she is."

Maya opened her mouth but Addie held up a finger. "Who she was, I know."

Maya stepped forward, pulling Addie into a gentle hug. "The police need to notify Lydia's parents before they'll release anything on the news, and the coroner needs to do an autopsy. We don't know what happened to her. You said it yourself."

"It wasn't bad mushrooms, Maya. She was murdered. You know it and I know it. Lydia Stevenson was murdered."

Do you like my surprise?

* * *

Addie and Maya served themselves massive bowls of cereal. Maya wolfed hers down while Addie pushed her cereal around through the milk, watching the little Os get progressively bigger as they absorbed the liquid. Every once in a while, Maya would reach out and pat her best friend on the arm, offer her a small smile.

"It's going to be okay," she said softly. "We're going to be okay."

Addie nodded and started to feel a modicum better. When they were back upstairs in Addie's room Maya pulled out a blouse, held it up to herself, and asked, "Can I pull this off?"

Addie cocked her head. "I think the question is 'Can your imaginary man pull that off?' And either way, the answer is no. You look like a funky banana. And besides, the tags are still on."

Maya's eyes flicked down to the still-attached price tag and bulged. "I'm pretty sure our house cost that much." She clenched her fist. "Damn you, parents, for choosing public service over brute capitalism!"

Addie snort-laughed to cover up her weird discomfort. Maya's parents were both in law enforcement: her mother, one year in as the chief of police, and her father, a homicide detective. The Garcia family had moved to Crescent City when Maya and Addie were freshmen at Hawthorne. They had nearly every class together, and—as Garcia and Gaines—sat next to each other in every alphabetically arranged one. Addie was shyer than shy, and at the time, so was Maya. She was a little chubby with Coke-bottle glasses and brown-black hair that should have been glossy and thick, but due to puberty was stringy and greasy. Addie was the tall and gangly one, the one who would look great on a runway if it weren't for her painful shyness, frizzy reddish hair, and inability to walk a straight line without stumbling over her own feet. Over the school year, the girls bonded over their shared awkwardness and kept it at bay by reading gobs of Gap Lake books and scrutinizing every detail. That first summer, Addie went away to a rich-kids summer camp in the Hamptons that she despised, while Maya grew three inches up in height and out in the chest area, got contacts, and developed an appreciation for boys who weren't on the page. Their friendship survived even as Maya tried desperately to drag her best friend into the three-dimensional world while Addie flourished online. Maya loved that Addie was real and down to earth when every stereotype told her to be a bitch; Addie loved everything about Maya—in particular, the fact that she knew about Addie's father but never, ever brought it up.

"Hey, your parents are heroes. That's pretty amazing."

"And your father could buy and sell this whole town."

Addie sucked her teeth. There were a lot of people in the town who would angrily agree with Maya—and argue that the reason Morton Gaines was walking around free was because he *did* buy the town—or at least the police department. She launched off the bed, grabbed the yellow blouse, and yanked off the price tag.

"You know what? You should wear this."

Maya pursed her lips. "I thought you said it made me look banana-y."

Addie shrugged. "I'm jealous, okay? I look ridiculous in that thing. You've got the boobs for it."

Maya grabbed her chest. "I do have great boobs."

"You're so weird."

"I am. And now I'm going to take a shower."

Addie rolled her eyes as Maya stomped across the floor and into the en suite bathroom. "God, your life is amazing!" she shouted—like she always did—before slamming the door and turning on the faucet. Addie grabbed her laptop from under the bed, clicked to her GapLakeLove site, and grinned at the ticker showing her page hits.

It was up by 1,500.

> PinUp55: I love, love, LOVE this site!
> PANDAPup: Best. Fanfic. EVER!!!!!
> Joni1: I swear this might be better than the Gap Lake books themselves.

Addie pulled up her story file and started writing.

Jordan knew she should be careful. Crystal Lanier was dead. Jordan straightened her shoulders as she walked through the forest, the smell of mud from the lake surrounding her. She could hear the suck from her shoes each time she stepped and she tried to block out the thudding of her heart. Suck, suck, thud. Suck, suck, thud.

A twig snapped behind her.

A car door slammed outside and Addie jumped, her laptop sliding off her thighs and onto the bed.

"Jeez!" She clutched at her racing heart, then laughed at herself, rolling up onto hands and knees and peering out her window. But the car wasn't in her driveway—it was in Colton's.

It was Spencer's car.

Addie scrambled off her bed and knelt in front of the window, low enough so that no one downstairs could see her peeking.

Spencer shifted the car into park but didn't move. Instead, he rested his forehead on the steering wheel. Addie pressed herself up a tiny bit more to get a better view of her crush, crumpled against his steering wheel in her next-door neighbor's driveway. *What is he doing here?*

They were friendly, Addie knew that. Everyone at Hawthorne High was pretty friendly. But Addie didn't know Spencer and Colton were the kind of friends who hung out. She shrunk back into the curtains as Colton came out the front door and knocked on Spencer's car door. They gave each other the obligatory boy head bob, then Spencer kicked open his car door.

She could make out something like "hey," then pressed her forehead against the cool glass as Spencer and Colton walked to the trunk of the car. Spencer pulled out a cardboard box. He handed it to Colton, piled a smaller one on top of that, and took another two himself.

Was Spencer moving in?

She was enrapt, watching Spencer and Colton's every move, heat racing across her body.

"You have the best shower," Maya said, opening the bathroom door in a cloud of steam. She had a towel turbaned around her head and another wrapped around her body as she slathered Addie's lotion on her arms. "I swear, ours is like a garden hose with a colander. What are you staring at?"

Addie sprang back from the window, landing with a hard thud on her butt. She blinked. "Nothing."

Maya's smile was wry. She crossed the room leaving wet footprints on the carpet. She picked at the curtains, peered out.

"You're spying on Colton. You can see directly into his bedroom from here. Dude, you're kind of a perv." She grinned and turned. "I must be rubbing off on you."

Addie grabbed her curtains and pulled them shut. "I wasn't spying on Colton." She paused for a beat, then licked her lips and lifted the corner of the curtain two inches. "I was actually spying on Spencer." She gestured with her chin. "His car is out there. It looked like he was moving in or something."

"Maybe he's just spending the night."

"They barely even talk, though. Isn't that weird?"

Maya shrugged. "They could be moving black market items and using Colton's room as a temporary holding spot."

Addie gaped.

"I'm kidding. You're nuts. Look"—Maya jutted her chin toward the window again—"Spencer's leaving. Mystery solved."

"That doesn't solve anything."

"Because there's nothing to solve, Sherlock Holmes." Maya took a handful of gummies from her stash and shoved them in her mouth. "Not everything that happens is some crazy mystery," she said with her mouth full.

"Don't you want to know what's in the boxes?"

Maya shrugged. "Nope. I want to know when I can start moving my boxes over."

Addie raised an eyebrow.

"I could so totally move in! Your dad won't even know I'm here. I'll just lay low here in the west wing." Her teeth were riddled with gummy bears.

NINE

"Oh. That's not good." Maya had her cell phone in her lap, a red gummy bear hanging out of her mouth.

"What's that?" Addie asked, wrinkling her nose at the dresses in her closet.

"Rumor mill. People are actually saying that they think Spencer had something to do with Lydia's murder."

The word *murder* was a cold black stone in Addie's gut. She could feel the color drain from her face, and the room started to spin. Addie didn't want this to be real. She didn't want any of this.

When she read Gap Lake mysteries, she secretly wished that something as interesting would happen in her town. When she wrote GapLakeLove, she lived in a world full of mystery and intrigue where everyone had some delicious secret, where every touch or conversation could mean nothing at all or a thousand wonderful, sinister things. She would close her laptop and drift off to sleep vaguely wishing that something would happen here in Crescent City, that there would be a big mystery, a big upheaval. But she never really wanted it.

"How do you even know that? We haven't been back to school."

Maya glanced up from her phone, then dangled it. "It's all over social media. People aren't out-and-out saying it but…"

"How can anyone think Spencer is responsible? He's just a kid—we're all just…" Addie let her sentence trail off.

"He put that one kid in a coma, you know."

Addie could feel the tension thrum through her, making her skin feel too hot, too tight.

"It was a concussion and it was an accident," Addie muttered under her breath. "Everyone knew it was an accident."

It had happened over a year ago when the Hawthorne boys' water polo team was in the semifinals against Crescent High. It was a tense game made worse by two weeks of trash talking and a rivalry that went back to the seventies. Then the game was tied with only four minutes left. Addie didn't remember much except some kind of skirmish, a lot of splashing, and the overwhelming crack of bone against concrete. Spencer was waist deep in the water looking dumbfounded as the Crescent High kid reeled backward. It seemed to go in slow motion at first, this guy sailing through the water, then everything moved very, very fast when his head hit the edge of the pool with a sickening thud. Addie remembered the collective *whoosh* of air from the astonished crowd; she remembered the sound of trainers *plunk*ing into the pool, pulling Spencer backward and pulling the Crescent kid out of the water. She had watched, transfixed, as they pounded his chest and patted his cheeks—and she had watched Spencer's face, drawn, tears mixed with beads of pool water as he shook his head and mouthed the words "I'm sorry. I'm so, so sorry," over and over again.

"So what do you think?"

Addie shook her head. "I don't know what to think, but I don't think Spencer had anything to do with it."

"Adds, he nearly killed someone during a water polo match."

"It was an accident. An *accident*, Maya. That doesn't make him a murderer."

"People kill for less."

Addie shook her head. "No, they don't. And not their girlfriends!"

Maya held up a finger. "He was her ex."

"So?"

"I'm just pointing out that there could have been something we don't know. I'm just saying! I am the daughter of cops, you know, and my parents always say there are five main reasons people kill: money, love, lust, revenge…" She frowned.

"And ex-girlfriends? I don't think so."

Maya held up her hands. "I'm just floating theories based on the myriad of misinformation being disseminated by unreliable sources through my phone."

"Your parents must be so proud."

"Come on. I'll drop you off on my way to work."

Addie stopped, seized by a memory.

The halls were empty, and Addie preferred it that way. The Hawthorne High campus was huge—building after nondescript building mirrored each other, all routed through with linoleum-filled halls that always smelled strongly of lemon and faintly of vomit. Between classes the halls were shoulder to shoulder with students, most of them spilling into the breezeways and quads. The whole thing made Addie vaguely claustrophobic, so she tried to time her bathroom runs during class time. It annoyed her teachers but kept her mildly sane.

Addie pushed through the ladies' room door and was immediately hit with the pungent scent of bleach and cheap perfume, the whirl of the overhead fan a monstrous growl above her, so strong that she almost didn't hear the whimpering.

All the stall doors were standing open and there was no one in the room.

"Hello?" she asked.

The whimpering stopped. Addie stopped, waited. The slight sound of a sniffle. She locked herself into one of the stalls, peed as quickly as possible, and stepped out, coming face-to-face with Lydia Stevenson.

"Oh." Addie licked her lips. "Hi. Sorry. I was just…" She looked around. "Peeing."

Lydia nodded, using her two pinkie fingers to wipe at her eyes. "I was just…" She bit her lip, then smiled thinly. "Crying like an idiot."

Addie didn't know what to do. "I'm sorry…should I go?"

Lydia shook her head, her long blond hair bobbing around her shoulders. "No, you have every right." Addie could tell the girl was trying to smile, was trying to force down the next wave of tears. Instinctively, Addie threw her arms around Lydia, engulfing her in a light hug.

"It's okay," she said quickly. "Whatever it is, it's okay."

Lydia stiffened for a half beat, shocked. When Addie went to straighten, she fell against her, her body racking in a fresh round of sobs. Addie stood there, rocking the most popular girl in school in her arms in the school bathroom, lightly patting her back and whispering, "shh."

She stood there until Lydia's sobs subsided, until she stepped away. Lydia smiled again, this one small and sheepish, her lipstick smeared, the edges of her nose a deep red. Her eyes were swollen and bloodshot, rimmed heavily with sleep and running mascara. Addie couldn't be certain but it looked like the puffiness and the bags went beyond an afternoon cry session.

"Are you okay, Lydia?"

Lydia waved at Addie, swallowed hard, then used both hands to gather her long hair into a ponytail. It was then that Addie could see the bruise on the underside of Lydia's bicep: a purple, pocked U shape. Lydia caught her staring and dropped her arms abruptly to her sides.

"I'm on my period," she said, shaking her head. "Everything either makes me cry or makes me super mad, you know?"

Addie nodded, pretending to understand while Lydia went to the sink, turned on the tap, and splashed water on her face. She glanced at her expression in the mirror and actually laughed, a high-pitched, tinkling sound that sounded wrong in Addie's ears, that looked wrong when matched with the red-nosed girl in the mirror. Lydia flicked the water from her hands, straightened what was left of her eyeliner with her pinkies, and spun to face Addie, holding out a hand with a single pinkie finger extended.

"Our little secret. Okay, Madison?"

Addie looked at the finger, at Lydia. "It's Addison."

Lydia's finger was still extended, her eyes glossy and glassy, staring *right through Addison as if she wasn't even there, but she didn't budge. Finally Addie extended her own hand, hooked Lydia's pinkie.*

"I guess," *she said.*

TEN

Maya sat back on Addie's bed, pulling a brush slowly through her glossy black hair.

Addie chewed the inside of her lip, pacing a bald spot in the carpet.

"Earth to Addison Gaines…"

"I have to tell you something."

Maya's eyes widened, and she waggled her eyebrows. "Big Wall Street secrets from your dad? You know I can't be trusted with money secrets."

"It's about Lydia Stevenson."

Maya's eyes cut across the bedroom, but she shrugged.

"Another theory? Shoot."

"I saw her in the bathroom about two weeks ago. She was crying. And she had"—Addie pulled up her arm, exposing the soft pale flesh and patting it gently—"a bite mark, right here."

"Are you sure that's what it was? I mean, it could have been…"

Addie shook her head, worried her bottom lip. "It was a U shape and it looked like little bubbles—like teeth. And if not teeth, then

I suppose it could have been finger marks, but isn't that just as bad? Someone gripped her hard enough to leave a mark? Or bit her?"

"You don't know for sure what it was."

"It looked like a bite mark, Maya. It looked like someone deliberately hurt her. And she was crying. What if whoever hurt her is the one who killed her?"

Maya paused for a beat, smoothing her ponytail. "Are you sure that's what it was? A bite mark?"

Addie looked away, tried to picture the mark on Lydia's arm. She had seen it for just a second—just a flash. Maybe she was wrong…? But then she saw the flit of something that went through Lydia's eyes: embarrassment, fear?

"I think someone was hurting her, Maya."

"I hate to tell you, but that's not looking any better for your boy, Spencer."

Addie narrowed her eyes. "He's not my boy. And you're being way too flippant."

"Or you're being overdramatic and a little bit pervy, staring at Lydia Stevenson's limbs."

"There was something on her wrist too."

Maya put her hands on her hips and yawned. "What?"

Addie nodded, thinking. "No, she definitely had a mark on her wrist too. I thought it was just a smudge of something, ink or something, but there was a definite bruise on her wrist."

Maya blew out a sigh. "Like she was handcuffed or something?"

"No." Addie clamped a hand over Maya's bony wrist, gripping her hard. "Like maybe someone just did this."

Maya's eyes flashed and she yanked her arm free, rubbing her fingertips along her wrist. "That hurt, you ass."

"So do you believe me?"

"No, not really."

"Maya!"

"Addie, Lydia had a little bruise on her arm and another one on her wrist. On any given day I've got bruises halfway down my body and I have no idea how they got there. I walk into things. I'm clumsy. Maybe Lydia was too."

"But you weren't crying in a bathroom, Maya. You didn't swear me to secrecy. It's weird. Hey—do you know why she and Spencer broke up?"

Maya shook her head. "They both just kept saying it was 'mutual.'" She made air quotes.

"Why the quotes?"

"No breakup is mutual."

"What if there was someone else?"

Maya shrugged. "What if?"

"No, Maya, really. What if they broke up because Lydia was seeing someone else? And maybe that was the person who was hurting her? I mean, Spencer wouldn't want it to get out that Lydia may have been cheating on him, so he would float the whole 'it was mutual' story."

"Or, Lydia could have cheated on Spencer, and Spencer caught her, which is why he bruised up her arm and bit her or whatever, and then he stalked her and finally killed her. Sorry, Adds, I'm not really seeing this work out in Spencer's favor."

Addie sucked in a deep breath. "Don't you think I could be just a little bit on to something?"

Maya crossed her arms in front of her chest and shook her head, lips pulled down in a grimace. "I think you're making a big deal out of nothing."

"Please just mention it to your dad, okay?"

Maya eyed Addie but eventually nodded. "I will, and when he tells me it's nothing you'll let it go, okay? Spencer, the bruise, Lydia's abusive mystery man?"

Addie wanted to dismiss it, wanted to believe that Maya was probably right. But there was something in Lydia's eyes—it was only there for a fleeting second, but it was there: a haunted look. A desperate look. And now Lydia Stevenson was dead.

ELEVEN

Addie and her father sat in the waiting room of the Crescent City Police Department. Morton Gaines was all business in a pressed gray sport jacket and a pale blue button-down with the collar open. He looked relaxed as he smiled and nodded to the officers who buzzed around the front vestibule.

Addie was another matter.

When she had woken that morning, she had stared into her closet for a good thirty minutes. *What did one wear to a police interview?*

For Addie, it wasn't her first. The first time, she was thirteen and had worn a stiff wool dress even though it was summer and a thousand degrees outside. She had worn white tights and black shoes and nodded silently when the police officers asked her questions about her father, about the speed of the car—questions that she couldn't answer. She was a child then, shaking on the bench while her father looked cool, and she was a young adult now—but she didn't feel any more confident.

"Addison?"

Maya's father was the same height as Addie's, but his shoulder span was a full inch wider and the stern set of his jaw put Addie on edge. Usually, she loved hanging out at Maya's house, loved when Detective Garcia would come home and tie on an apron and give Maya lessons on making something like his signature enchiladas. It grossed Maya out supremely, but Addie loved everything about it. Today, in the police department, Maya's dad was gone and Detective Garcia—stern, unsmiling—took his place. He was wearing dark pants and a white button-down shirt, his Crescent City detective badge slung on a leather cord around his neck. Addie sucked in a breath when he turned, his leather holster and gun at the ready.

"I'm here," Addie said, standing, then feeling immediately stupid. "I mean, ready."

Her father stood next to her, putting out a hand for the detective. "I'm sorry we have to meet again under these circumstances, Roger."

Detective Garcia shook Morton Gaines's hand, nodded curtly, and offered Addie a smile that was meant to be reassuring, but that just put her more on edge. For the first time that she could remember, Detective Garcia seemed to stare Addie down.

"These are just routine questions, correct, Detective? I mean, I don't need my lawyer present or anything…" Addie's father's voice was spun sugar, but it made her stomach churn.

A lawyer?

"I'm not—I'm not in trouble or anything, right?"

Detective Garcia shook his head, waved his arm dismissively.

"No, of course not. I just wanted to get Addie's statement in a more official capacity."

Addie's tongue went heavy in her mouth as she followed the detective and her father into a claustrophobia-inducing room on the second floor of the police station.

"Now, Addie, I don't want you to worry about anything. You're not in any trouble. We're just going to take your statement about exactly what you saw on Friday night."

She licked her Sahara-dry lips. "I already talked to the officer who was there."

Detective Garcia offered Addie and her father a seat and shuffled some papers. "Yep, I have your statement right here. Let's just go over it, shall we?"

There was a beat of silence. The temperature in the room seemed to ratchet up ten degrees, and Addie picked at her T-shirt.

"Do you want me to start?"

"Just tell me what you saw that night, okay?"

Addie cleared her throat, looked at her father and then at the detective, and repeated the whole story. Detective Garcia would look from her to the papers in his hand and back again, bobbing his head kindly.

"Uh-huh, and it says here you mentioned someone named R. J. Rosen?"

"Is that someone from your school, honey?"

Embarrassment burned Addie's cheeks and she shook her head. "No. R. J. Rosen is an author. He writes the Gap Lake books."

"And why did you bring him up, Addison?"

She swallowed, glancing at her father, who nodded encouragingly. "It just—the night was weird. It was like out of a book. It was like out of one of the Gap Lake mysteries, and I just mentioned that."

Detective Garcia nodded his hand, scrawled something down on a piece of paper. His expression didn't change. "Is that everything?"

No, Addie wanted to say. It's not. But what could she say? Her favorite author had sent her a story and it read just like the murder scene?

She paused, worrying her bottom lip. "Something you want to say, Addison?" her father asked.

Addie shifted her weight. "What if—is it possible that someone wanted to make this look like a murder from a book?"

Detective Gaines stared Addie down but seemed to be considering. "Like acting something out?" he asked finally.

"Like that," Addie said, her heart thundering in her chest. "Or like a copycat."

Detective Garcia and Addie's father shared a look over Addie's head, the detective's lips quirking up in a half smile. "It's possible you read too many books, Addie."

Addie followed her father down the steps and through the waiting room where Colton was sitting on one of the hard plastic chairs, staring straight ahead. His palms were on his knees, knuckles white. His eyes flicked to Addie when she walked through and she tried to offer a smile, but her lips were so dry she was sure they would crack. Instead, she offered him a half wave that he didn't return.

She wasn't supposed to see her friends at the police station.

She wasn't supposed to be questioned about a murder.

Addie grabbed her cell phone to talk to Maya but there was already a message there.

TheRealRJRosen:

And so the story begins...

TWELVE

"I feel weird about this, don't you?" Addie asked, shifting the blanket she was carrying from one hip to the other.

Maya shrugged. "I guess, but life—"

"Don't say 'imitates art.'"

"I wasn't going to. I was going to say life goes on. I mean, it's really terrible about what happened to Lydia but…what are we supposed to do? Stay cooped up until we graduate? It's not like there's a curfew or anything, and it's not like anything is going to happen out here. We're at the boardwalk about to watch a movie so, A, no place to hide and B, look around you. Everyone in school is here."

Maya was right. The entire cracked parking lot of the boardwalk was clogged with cars, the majority of them bearing Hawthorne High parking passes or Fighting Hornet stickers.

"There's Colton. Let's go over there."

Addie followed Maya, who immediately melded into a group of teenagers. Before the song blasting out of someone's car stereo changed, the blanket Addie was carrying was spread on the sand,

and Addie was handed a red plastic cup filled with cheap beer. The scent alone turned her stomach, but she held it anyway, grateful to have something to do with her hands.

Maya was right; the entire student body of Hawthorne High spilled off the boardwalk and littered the beach. The police force wasn't there, but Addie could see a squad car with its low beams on parked at the top of one of the sand dunes, and she surreptitiously tipped her Solo cup over and dribbled half her beer into the sand.

"Watering the sand?" Spencer asked, a small smile playing at the edges of his lips.

Addie startled and tucked her cup behind her back. "Oh, hey. I didn't know you were here."

He shrugged, his gaze sweeping over the dunes. "I guess I'm kind of keeping a low profile."

"Are you…are you okay?"

There was a long pause that Addie wanted to fill with mindless blather, but she held back. Spencer kicked at the wet ring in the sand from Addie's beer. "I don't really know how I'm supposed to feel."

Addie nodded because there wasn't anything else to say. Then, "I—I know you're innocent."

Color flushed Spencer's cheeks. "Thanks?"

"I mean—I just know there were rumors. I didn't believe them though."

Spencer nodded. "They were just rumors. The police questioned me, but I don't know anything." His voice caught and Addie looked up, blinked through the darkness. Spencer's eye were glistening like he was holding back tears. "I wish I knew something. The truth was…Lydia and I had barely talked in weeks." He cleared his throat. "She had already moved on."

Addie straightened. "She had a new boyfriend?"

Spencer dug his hands in his pockets and cocked his head. "I think she had one before we broke up."

There were rumors that Crystal Lanier was cheating on Declan Levy and that's why he killed her, Addie thought. She shook herself. That was a book. This was real life. "Do you want the rest of my beer?"

He offered a shy little half smile that did something to Addie. Her heartbeat sped up. Her breathing slowed—but this time, it was a good thing.

"No thanks. I hate that stuff."

"You prefer something harder?"

Spencer shook his head. "I guess. 7 UP is hard, right?"

Addie wrinkled her brow. "You don't drink? Like, at all?"

"Is that weird?" He took a few steps across the sand, and Addie found herself following behind him.

"Not weird at all, just surprising. I don't actually drink either."

Spencer jutted his chin. "I see. You're just into watering the sand?"

Heat broke over the tops of Addie's ears. "They handed me a drink. I just…"

Spencer shrugged, but his expression was kind. "I get it. Peer pressure and all that. Want to walk?"

Now it was Addie's turn to smile. "I thought we were."

They went a few more feet, walking in silence until the din of students on the sand was a low roar and the lights from the boardwalk were nothing but splashes of color in the distance. The horizon was varying shades of dark.

"My dad's an alcoholic." Spencer volunteered. "Or I guess he is now. Once you see your pops facedown in his own vomit, you kind of lose the urge to party even if everyone else is doing it."

Addie could only nod even though she wanted to tell Spencer she knew exactly how he felt. She hadn't seen her father facedown in his own vomit—but she had seen him in handcuffs. She had seen his face drawn and gaunt after weeks of back-and-forth with lawyers and cops. She had seen the smug smile on his face when he walked free, the drunk driving offense expunged from his record.

"That's got to be rough," was all she said.

Though it was dark, a bit of silver moonlight washed over them, enough that she could study Spencer's reflection, could see the hard set of his jaw when he swallowed. She watched his Adam's apple bob.

"Yeah, it is."

They were silent for a beat, the hum of the night air and the crash of the waves between them. "So, Addison Gaines. What's your deal? What are you doing out here?"

"It's a bonfire. It's not really an invitation thing, right?"

"No, I was just—just trying to start a conversation. Badly, obviously. Just wondering who the real Addie is."

Addie couldn't hide her bemused grin. "'The real Addie?' Wow, that sounds—that sounds ridiculous. The real me loved pink when

I was a kid, hates beer, and has a massive aversion"—she picked up her foot and shook it—"to getting sand in my socks."

He raised a shoulder in a sort of half shrug. "Ah. So the real story begins."

Addie's stomach dropped to her knees. She stopped walking, turned to face Spencer. "What did you just say?"

She could see Spencer's eyes widen, could see the bloom on his cheeks. "Nothing, I wasn't trying to hit on…I was just being—"

"No," Addie shrugged. "No, that was weird of me. I was just asking—" She pulled out her phone and pointed to it as if that would explain everything. She clapped a hand over her face. "Never mind. I'm lame and kind of a freak. All of this"—she gestured to the world as a whole—"I'm kind of on the edge."

Spencer let out a half chuckle. "You and me both. And I didn't mean that to sound…I mean, I feel…Lydia was my—"

Addie shook her head. "Truce, okay? You and me, we both say really stupid things, but they die right here and now, okay?"

There was a long, awkward beat as what Addie said hung between them.

"I didn't mean die." She licked her dry lips. "I shouldn't have said that."

Spencer held out a hand, then curled his fingers back, offering only his pinkie. His smile was small and shy, and it melted Addie's heart. "Truce, okay?"

THIRTEEN

It was midnight by the time Addie got into bed. She yanked the covers up around her, worried that she wouldn't be able to sleep. Her father was in the next room, and the house was deathly still. Addie was tired, but every time she tried to close her eyes she saw Lydia, glaring at her.

Addie had a crush on Spencer. Addie had a crush on a dead girl's ex-boyfriend.

Who people think might be responsible for her murder.

No, he wasn't. That wasn't right. She savored the night, holding it against her, replaying the sweet conversation, the sweet warmth of Spencer near her. Before she knew it, her eyes were fluttering and she began to dream.

Addie could see her feet, her toenails painted Easter-egg blue. She was barefoot, those blue toenails digging into sand so pale it was almost white.

Where was she?

She spun, taking in her surroundings: mile-high pine trees shrugging toward the sky. The white sand beach, half-lined with an ancient looking boardwalk. A café that looked like it was part of the scenery. She squinted. GAP LAKE EAT AND DRINK *was painted on the side of the stucco wall in faded red paint, right above the phrase, "Get in here!" Addie turned. The lake was in front of her, the cold water barely lapping at her toes.*

Instinctively, Addie knew that it was junior cut day, that the banks were about to be choked with Gap Lake High students and that—yes, right there—over her left shoulder there was a clearing. Two girls in beach chairs, a cooler between them.

Crystal and Jordan.

Behind her, Addie knew that Declan Levy was talking to Poppy, the summer worker who died in the first chapter of book one. She knew that Jordan would discover the pair while Crystal stayed at the lake drinking an energy drink. Addie heard the pop of the top. She watched as Jordan—exactly as she had pictured her each time she read the books—stood up, dusted sand from the back of her cutoff shorts, and walked to GAP LAKE EAT AND DRINK. *Addie wanted to stop her, to sit down next to Crystal and explain what was about to happen. But there was someone already sitting in Jordan's vacated chair.*

Lydia Stevenson.

She was wearing short shorts and a bikini top, rubbing sunscreen on her long, already tanned arms. She and Crystal didn't seem to notice each other.

"Lydia?" Addie blinked at the girl. "What are you doing here? This is Gap Lake. You're not—you're real."

Lydia stopped what she was doing and pulled her sunglasses a half inch down her perfect little nose to stare at Addie. "Am I?"

Addie blinked. "You shouldn't be here anyway. Jordan is going to come back and then—" *Then what?* Addie racked her brain, trying to remember the scene in the book. Whatever it was, she knew it didn't have Lydia Stevenson in it.

"You're weird," Lydia said, batting at the air as she stood. She took a step closer to Addie so that they were nearly nose to nose. "There's one thing you should keep in mind, Addison. If a character comes into a book in an unexpected place, it's usually for very good reason." Lydia slid off her sunglasses and dropped them onto the sand, turned her back on Addie and the still-silent Crystal, and began to walk down the beach toward the lake. Addie had to run to keep up with her.

"What is that supposed to mean?"

But Lydia kept walking, taking slow, deliberate steps that left two-inch-deep imprints in the sand. When she got to the water's edge she turned and smiled at Addie, her lips blood red and heart shaped. "One more thing you should keep in mind too," she whispered before snaking a hand behind Addie's neck. "Life imitates art."

Addie didn't have time to blink. She didn't have time to consider what Lydia was saying to her before the water was lapping over her lips, rushing down her throat. It was in her nose, and when she tried to open her eyes everything was waterlogged. She saw the sky above her and she tried desperately to claw at it, but Lydia still had ahold of her neck. She was going down, she and Lydia both, and when she finally stopped struggling, that's when she saw it: Lydia, in front of her, eyes wide open. Bright, but something about them was unsettling— unseeing. She was deep underwater, her hair floating around her, her perfect mouth open in a silent scream.

Addie's own screams woke her up. She was gasping and coughing, a sheen of sweat making her nightshirt stick to her back and dampening her sheets. "Oh, oh God."

She had dreamed about Gap Lake. No—she had dreamed about Lydia Stevenson. Dead. Drowned in the lake. Addie shook herself and sat up, pressing the soles of her feet into the heavily piled carpet. She needed to feel something solid underneath her. She needed to know that she wasn't going to drown.

"Everything okay in here, kiddo?" Addie's father poked his head into her doorway, brows knitted. "Did I hear you scream?"

Suddenly, Addie was embarrassed. She was a little girl who had had a nightmare—bad enough to scare her into a cold sweat. She shook her head. "I'm okay, Dad. Just a dumb dream."

Mr. Gaines grinned, cheeks pushing up, making his hazel eyes crinkle. Addie liked the effect; she realized it had been a long time since she saw her father smile. "Let me guess—you stayed up late reading those River Run mysteries, huh?"

Addie felt annoyance flutter in her chest. "Gap Lake, Dad. And no."

"Anyway, breakfast in five."

Addie waited to hear her father's steps on the stairs before she stepped in the shower, the spray of water hitting her with a start.

Lydia Stevenson, underwater.

Addie, being pulled under, the water sealing her lips, swirling until it reached her nostrils. She was coughing, struggling to breathe again, as the steam from the hot water rose and pressed against her chest.

She was drowning again.

Addie pushed her way out of the shower, grabbing a towel and rubbing it over her face.

This is crazy, she said to herself. *I had a bad dream. I had a bad dream because I read a scary book and watched the news and that's all there is to it. I'm not going to drown in the shower.*

She knew it was true, but she made sure to double-tighten the faucet anyway.

FOURTEEN

On Monday morning, Addie's father had the refrigerator doors open and was balancing a stack of disposable cartons in one hand while wrestling an orange juice carton from between two pizza boxes with the other.

"We should really clean out the fridge."

Addie took the orange juice and the top two disposable containers. "We really should learn how to cook."

Mr. Gaines frowned. "I thought you loved Louisa's cooking."

Louisa came to the house four days a week to cook and clean, and make sure that Addie was doing something that looked like homework after school while her father worked late. The days she didn't come, she packed the fridge with disposable containers of cheese-laden casseroles and macaroni salads. She was an old lady who lived on carbs and cheese food. She was kind and always warm to Addie and her father, but she wasn't Addie's mom.

Nineteen days after Addie's mom left—when Addie was still counting her mom's absence in days—her father pulled out the chair across from her, steepled his fingers, and said, "We need to bring someone in."

Addie had no idea what that meant, but it began a series of women coming through their door—housekeepers and glorified babysitters, women who wanted a crack at becoming the next Mrs. Gaines, girls barely out of college who told her dad they just "loved kids" but who regarded Addie as some sort of competition. Addie hated the first one, a plump woman who filled the house with apple-pie spice and sang unsettling hymns. The second couldn't pour a bowl of cereal and had boobs up to her chin. The third, fourth, and fifth were gone within weeks. Addie couldn't remember what number Louisa was, but she knew enough not to get close.

"I do, but sometimes it might be nice to, you know, make something ourselves."

Mr. Gaines did one of those frown head bobs that Addie knew meant he was considering the offer. "I guess we could try that. But until then—hash brown casserole or French toast casserole?"

"I'll stick with cereal," she said, pulling a bowl from the cabinet. Her father flicked on the television. That was another thing that had changed since her mother left: now, whenever Addie and her father were alone, he flicked on the television, never actually caring what show was on. He didn't even bother to channel surf most days, just clicked on the set and let whatever chatter was already playing fill up the otherwise silent house. This morning, it was the news.

"Hey, honey, isn't that your school?"

Addie didn't have to look at the screen to know it was. Her

stomach sank as the reporter looked directly into the camera, brows knitted, jaw clenched.

"Seventeen-year-old Lydia Stevenson was found deceased at Hawthorne High late Friday night."

The word *deceased* sent a chill through Addie.

Teenagers weren't supposed to be deceased.

Mr. Gaines turned in his chair, eyebrows raised. "Are you doing okay?"

Addie felt the anger swell low in her belly. She and Maya had found Lydia. She had been besieged by a parade of police officers and shivered under the covers next to Maya, and now her father was concerned.

Addie nodded slowly, looking down at the cereal and milk in her bowl. Already it looked like sludge, and her stomach churned. She pushed the bowl aside. "I'm doing okay. I just want things to go back to normal."

The news anchor went on to report everything that they already knew. She went through the series of events, just as Addie herself had described—and witnessed—them, then added: *"The last person to see Lydia alive was her seventeen-year-old boyfriend. Police aren't saying that he's a suspect in this case at this time, but have created a hotline for any leads."* Again, they didn't mention him by name. Again, they made it sound like he was guilty of something. Addie reached forward and flicked off the television set.

"Can we just have a little quiet, please, Dad?"

Mr. Gaines reached across the table, resting his hand on Addie's. "Maybe we should call Dr. Britton."

Ice water shot through Addie's veins, and her tongue felt heavy in her mouth. Dr. Britton was the therapist her father had sicced on her after her mother left and after the accident. She was a prim woman who wore pencil skirts that molded to her perfect curves. She had thick brown hair that hung to the middle of her back and glossy brown eyes punctuated by perfect brows that had a practiced look of perma concern. Addie hated her the moment she walked into the office. Dr. Britton was a perfect specimen behind a huge mahogany desk backed by degrees written in fancy script from a half-dozen universities and institutions. She wanted to talk to Addie about her feelings: how Addie felt inadequate and unloved; she batted her eyes and said she could relate.

Addie doubted it.

"No, Dad."

"I know you hung out with Maya, but going back to school could be kind of a trigger, you know?"

Trigger.

That word.

Dr. Britton had used it to talk about her mother leaving. Addie could still feel the anger surge through her body. Her mother wasn't a trigger. Her mother leaving wasn't a trigger. The man who had called the doctor, who had schmoozed her up while Addie got a soda from the machine, was the trigger. The car he pulled up to take Addie home in was a trigger.

"If you're scared, if you'd like to take some time and stay home from school today…"

Addie almost felt hopeful. It almost felt like old times, when she was a kid and her dad would hold her hand, build her a blanket fort, and hole up with her in her bedroom to keep watch for monsters. Except now, the monster was real.

"Maybe—"

"I can't stay with you, of course, but I bet Louisa would enjoy the company."

Louisa.

Addie brought her untouched cereal bowl to the sink and dumped it, watching as the cereal and milk swelled in the sink, then clogged the drain. "I'll be okay, Dad. Thanks anyway."

There was a long pause. "Do you want a ride today?"

Addie kept her eyes on her shoes as she shook her head in a sharp "no." She could hear her father's annoyed sigh. "You could drive yourself, you know."

FIFTEEN

"Actually, Maya is on her way." She offered him a bared-teeth grin, shimmying by the garage door that held her father's car and hers, side by side. Addie had had her license since the day she turned sixteen, and the new car was a peace offering, her father's way of trying to quell her anxiety, but it had the opposite effect. Every time she got behind the wheel, each time she rested her palms against the buttery soft leather, she could feel the anxiety swell in her chest. Sweat broke out above her upper lip, and her father's accident played on an endless loop, a black-and-white, terrifying film strip.

She sat in the passenger seat, her father behind the wheel. He stank of bourbon and smoke and Addie pretended not to notice. He drove carefully at first, holding the wheel with both hands, knuckles white. But then he started talking, laughing, gesturing wildly, and Addie kept her eyes on the road, kept focusing on the asphalt flying by. At first it was fine, but her eyes flicked to the speedometer: 25, 30, 35, 40. She watched as the front of the car veered to one side, then lurched to the other, swallowing up the double yellow lines.

"Dad, slow down."

"I'm barely doing thirty, hon."

Even now, Addie could feel the heat burst in her chest, the starburst of pain that thudded behind her eyes as the speedometer climbed and her father's voice went from his usual chatter to a boisterous blather. He took one hand off the wheel and chucked her under the chin. She could smell the cigar smoke on his fingertips; she could taste the biting scent of alcohol on his breath.

"Dad, you're drunk."

"I had one drink, Addison."

She shook her head, grinding her shoulders into the soft leather of the car seat, grounding the soles of her feet. She checked her seat belt, feeling the thick weave pressing hard against her waist, her chest. She was sure if she really looked, she could see the belt move against her heart as it slammed into her rib cage. Addie's lips went dry as her palms started to sweat. She clamped her eyes shut, refusing to look at the climbing speedometer, at the double yellow lines that wiggled and slashed across the asphalt.

"Dad, please."

They were in town, nearing the square. Addie could see the awnings from the farmer's market about a mile ahead. She willed her father to turn, begged God to let the car fail, make the engine fall out, the road suddenly close.

No such luck.

Addie couldn't tell if it was the hum of the road or the rush of blood in her temples, but she had to scream, had to make her father hear her.

"Dad, slow down. You have to slow down!"

He didn't answer. He didn't even look at her. He just kept blinking at the road, squinting like it was dark instead of broad daylight. She considered grabbing the wheel. She thought about gripping the little leather teardrop that hung from the key chain and yanking, but it was already too late.

They were in the town square.

The farmer's market awnings were on either side of them. People were scattering, and a table exploded over the hood, vegetables pelting the windshield. No one was hurt, but the humiliation and radiating fear pulsed through Addie for years to come, choking her every time she got behind the wheel, becoming too much when the engine purred.

Maya honked twice, and Addie was pulled from her daymare.

"You know Maya could ring the doorbell like a civilized person."

Addie spun, rage engulfing her. A civilized person doesn't drive drunk in the middle of the day. A civilized person doesn't pick his daughter up from junior high with bourbon on his breath.

A civilized person wouldn't roar through a marketplace, freaking out his kid.

She hiked her backpack onto her shoulder and grabbed an apple. "Whatever, Dad," she muttered under her breath.

"What's that, dear?"

"I'll see you after school."

Her father engulfed her in a bear hug and Addie wanted to forgive him. She wanted to soften into his hug like she had done a million times before she turned eleven, before the police came to her house. But she couldn't. She gave him a cursory pat on the shoulder instead, extricated herself, and zipped out the front door and into Maya's perennially on-the-way-to-breaking-down Honda Accord.

"Hey," Maya said, turning the radio down a half turn.

"Hey." Addie sat down hard, belted herself in, let the still-loud thud of the Accord's bass thrum through her body. "I love this song."

"'Death to Sea Monkeys,'" Maya said with a double eyebrow waggle. She zoomed out of the driveway fast enough for Addie to grab the dashboard, go completely white.

"Sorry," Maya said, her cheeks blushing a fire pink. "Forgot."

Maya was the only one who knew that Addie was in the car that day. She was the only person that Addie had ever told; the only person who knew that simply being in a car ratcheted her anxiety to nauseating levels. And Maya usually did her best, when Addie was in the car at least, to drive slowly and safely, obeying all traffic laws and keeping both hands on the wheel like she was constantly taking her driving test.

"Hey," she said, yanking her sunglasses down her nose. "Isn't that Spencer's car?"

Addie turned in her seat, frowned. "Yeah, yeah I think it is."

"What's he still doing at Colton's house?"

Addie shrugged.

"Maybe Colton's fixing Spencer's computer or something."

"Probably."

Maya raised an eyebrow. "You'd better hope that's all it is."

Addie crossed her arms in front of her chest. "Just drive, Uber, would you?"

Maya made the left-hand turn onto Educational Parkway, then

slammed on the brakes, nearly sending Addie into the dashboard. Her heart hammered in her chest, her fingers gripping the cracked vinyl stretched across the glove box.

"Holy shit!"

"I'm so sorry," Maya said, licking her lips nervously. "There's never this much traffic out here."

Cars were spilling out of the U-shaped parking lot in front of the high school, backing up onto the street. They were inching at a snail's pace, blocking the entrance to the student lot. Addie glanced at the glowing numbers on the dash. "If we have to sit here much longer, we're going to be late."

Maya raised a single shoulder. "Which wouldn't be the worst thing in the world."

Addie glanced at her friend.

"I have AP bio first period. And I may not have studied for the test."

"Do you ever?"

"No, but I almost always feel guilty about it. Usually. That counts, right?"

"Sure." Addie rolled down the window, cupping her eyes with her hands. "There's something going on. No one's moving in the admin lot."

Maya did a quick maneuver around a Chrysler that had stopped in the road, the doors kicked open as students ambled out and picked through traffic.

"There are cop cars up front."

Addie followed her gaze, her eyes focusing on the two

black-and-whites. One was at the front of the cavalcade of cars, the other had pulled directly onto campus, was sitting with doors open in the quad. Addie felt the blood drain from her face as a cold chill went down her spine.

SIXTEEN

There was another message on her cell phone when Addie sat down in her next class. She glanced up, cutting her eyes across the room. Mr. Hoover wasn't looking at her directly, but he wasn't exactly *not* looking at her either. She slid the phone down the arm of her sweater and swiped, staring at the message.

TheRealRJRosen:

I've been watching you…

Addie's breath caught sharp and hard. She could feel sweat bead between her shoulder blades, her heart thundering in her chest.

"What?" she muttered.

"Did you say something, Ms. Gaines?"

Addie shook her head, hoping the look of shock wasn't registering with him. "No, Mr. Hoover. Sorry."

She cut her eyes back to her phone, desperate to see what R. J. Rosen said.

I've been watching you?

She thought of Lydia, of Friday night, the way the journalism room stank of mildew. She thought of the text R. J. had sent her and shot her hand up in the air.

"Mr. Hoover? I don't feel so well. Can I—"

Mr. Hoover nodded his head sharply, bent over, and scribbled something on a pink Post-it note. Addie shoved her phone farther into her sleeve and zipped up the aisle, grabbing the note and stuffing it in her back pocket.

"Thanks," she muttered on her way out.

"Hey," Addie spun when Kelly Weiss called out to her in the hallway. Kelly was the only sophomore on the school newspaper. She was a whole head shorter than Addie with a pixie cut done in three shades of purple that made her thick black eyebrows stand out like caterpillars. Addie couldn't have pulled it off, but the look was actually cute on the girl.

"Sorry, I've got to—"

"Just wanted to say I love, love, love your new site. And your new fanfic? I might actually be a bigger Addie Gaines fan than I am a R. J. Rosen fan."

Addie stopped in her tracks, pride swelling through her. "Really?"

Kelly pumped her head. "You're really, really good, Addie. If we could get another story for the school newspaper, it would be amazing."

Addie bit her lower lip. "I guess I could do that." She grinned. "Really though? I usually just do one a semester."

Kelly shrugged. "You're kind of the shit, and mystery is all the rage." She slapped a black fingernailed hand over her mouth.

"Omigod! That sounded really terrible. I didn't mean—it's just that people like a kind of escape, you know?"

"And you can only watch so many kittens on YouTube."

Kelly smiled, cheeks still flushed pink. "So you'll do it?"

Addie's phone pinged from her sleeve and the pride she felt disappeared with a pinprick.

"Let me think about it, okay? I just—I've got a lot of work to do on the GapLakeLove blog and homework. I'll think about it, okay?"

Kelly nodded so hard that short, purple wisps of hair bounced up and down. "Do it. Please."

"'Kay," Addie turned, sliding her phone out of her sleeve and going directly to the bathroom. She began to read again.

TheRealRJRosen:

> I've been watching you and your blog, and wow! Your numbers look terrific. I can't tell you how much I appreciate your being a part of this launch! The next thing I'd like you to do is post a story on your site as a teaser. I'd like you to post this tonight at 9:00 p.m. What do you think?

Addie wanted to say no. She wanted to ask R. J. Rosen who he was, what he meant by his "surprise," but Maya and Colton's words came back to her: she was being stupid. She was being paranoid and freaky and R. J. Rosen was talking to her about a book that had nothing to do with what happened to Lydia.

But the mildew smell…

Meant nothing, Addie told herself firmly.

Fingertips on fire, she plunked across the keyboard on her phone.

AddieGaines:

That sounds amazing! I am so happy and honored to host. I'll post this at the stroke of nine!

Addie sent off the note then felt immediately stupid.

"Who says 'at the stroke of nine'?" She rolled her eyes, then started to read.

It took a second for Jordan's eyes to adjust to the darkness. Her head was throbbing, a one-two sucker punch to the temple, and her jaw ached. When she rubbed it, the pain radiated in a starburst and she coughed, a gush of blood flooding her gums. She tried to remember what had happened, but the pain in her head was taking over everything. She tried to breathe, sucking in sharp, shallow breaths that made her rib cage scream. Little by little, it came back to her.

Crystal.

Jordan winced, remembering the way the water lapped at her toes, feeling the mud that oozed under her feet, made the soft sucking sound as she nudged herself toward the edge of the lake. There was something floating there—

Her stomach dropped.

*There was some*one *floating there.*

Long, marble legs. Gauzy white fabric. A halo of blue-black hair.

Crystal.

Addie looked up from her phone, heart pounding in her throat. "Jordan was there! Jordan was there when Crystal died!" she whispered.

She dipped her head and continued to read.

Jordan pressed her eyes shut, willing herself to remember more. She saw Crystal—she knew she'd been found, so why was she remembering…?

The hand.

She felt the weight, the fingers on her arms, on her shoulders—around her throat.

"No, no—" she started to claw in the darkness, even though no one was there as she remembered. Fingers around her throat, throwing her so easily. Her palms hit the water first; she slapped and splashed, but the hands around her neck didn't loosen and she was going down, down, desperate for breath, for air when her face broke the surface of the water. The water was in her mouth, swirling through her nose. She was coughing, sputtering, but every breath was waterleaden. Jordan opened her eyes, did her best to turn, to arch, to kick, but the person who held her was too strong—too familiar. He shadowed her every move, easily pushing her down through the water.

This is what it feels like to die, she thought. This is what it felt like for Crystal.

The bell rang and Addie jumped, nearly dropping her phone in the toilet. She replayed the passage over and over again in her head. Jordan was there when Crystal died and someone tried to drown her too. She rubbed her chin. But who? The big mystery of Gap Lake was who killed Crystal and why—and if her friends would figure it out before they were next.

Addie immediately began writing back:

AddieGaines:

> OMG! It's so exciting! I love it!
> Thank you so much for sending it!

His response was just as quick.

TheRealRJRosen:

> I'm glad you like it. Don't forget to
> post it tonight!

She was grinning, fingertips cold as she stepped into the hall. She had inside information into Gap Lake and she had to tell someone! But one look around shattered Addie back down to solid reality. Lydia Stevenson wasn't a character in a book. She wouldn't turn up three hundred pages later.

This wasn't a story.

SEVENTEEN

Maya was waiting for Addie when the bell rang after second period.

"You are, like, the slowest person ever." She narrowed her eyes. "Tell me you were all swept up in Spencer during class."

"Right, because right after World History, I have Human Anatomy and they totally wanted volunteers so you know, me and Spencer."

Maya smiled. "You're gross and I love you."

"I get it from you."

"That's *why* I love you. You're like my little moldable lump of clay." Maya looked over both shoulders. "It's creepy around here again."

The usual din and chatter of the students was a low murmur again, the crowd in the halls slow and careful. Eyes seemed to be darting, people seemed to be whispering, and no one was smiling.

"I know. I can't exactly put my finger on it, but it's...I don't know, creepy somehow?"

Maya hitched her chin. "Can you put your finger on that?"

Addie followed her gaze, out the wide open front window to the horseshoe-shaped drive outside. Police cars. Two of them. Their lights were flashing, cutting red, white, and blue stripes through the hall, but there was no sound.

"I wonder why they're here," Maya said.

Addie looked at her best friend. "If I weren't so freaked out, I'd make a joke about you watching too much TV."

"Hey, I'm thinking of following ole Ma and Pa's footsteps into law enforcement."

"I thought you were thinking of going into living off me? Or—*gross*—marrying my dad? I prefer you in a law enforcement career to either of those by the way."

Maya tried to smile, but her eyes were fixed on the police cars as they crept into the parking lot, filling each space, then overflowing in an organized line like a series of black-and-white Tic Tacs.

"What do you think they want?"

"Ladies and gentlemen." The overhead announcement speaker crackled overhead. "Please don't be alarmed at the police cars lining up out front of the school. This is just a precautionary measure and you are to go about your day as if they are not here."

"Really?" Maya crossed her arms in front of her chest. "A fellow student is dead, every cop within a hundred-mile radius is on our front lawn, and I'm supposed to do biology? Wrong."

Normally, Addie would agree with her best friend. But she had stopped looking at the police cars, had stopped listening to Principal Johnson talking overhead. She was looking at Spencer Cohen, right in front of her. He was transfixed on the police exiting their cars out front. He was gripping his backpack straps so hard his knuckles had gone white, and all the color had drained from his face.

Strangely—instinctively—Addie wanted to go to him. She didn't know what she'd say, exactly. She didn't know if she would comfort him or ask his side of the story, but something inside her was drawn to him looking so scared and so small among the Hawthorne High kids swarming around him. But her cell phone pinged.

No one ever called her when she was in school except her father for emergencies.

Addie looked at her phone.

Or R. J. Rosen.

The familiar zing of excitement from seeing R. J. Rosen's name on Addie's phone was gone, choked out by the pure weirdness of the day. Lydia Stevenson was dead. Hawthorne High was flooded with police cars and uniformed officers. And Spencer Cohen looked guilty.

"Hey," Colton said, shaking Addie back to the here and now. "Cops"—he shuddered—"always freak me out."

Addie gulped. "This whole thing is freaking me out."

"I think I'm going to go be freaked out over at Starbucks," Maya said.

"Brave girl," Colton said with a light shrug.

"You mean because of Lydia?" Addie tried to sound nonchalant.

Colton's eyes were saucer-wide. "You didn't hear?"

"Hear what?"

"The cops are here because they found Lydia's car."

EIGHTEEN

Something cold hardened in the pit of Addie's stomach. She tried to blink, to swallow furiously, to command her body to do something other than stand there like a freaky lump. "I didn't even know Lydia's car was missing."

Colton shrugged. "Me neither. But I guess it wasn't in the parking lot the other night and...you know, wasn't at home or whatever."

"So did...the person who hurt Lydia. Did he steal it or something?"

Another shrug from Colton. "They didn't say but they found the car. It was out by the Percolation Ponds."

Addie's tongue went heavy in her mouth. The "Perc Ponds"—so called by Hawthorne High students for as long as Addie knew— were a group of shallow ponds in a wooded area less than a mile from the school. They were in an unincorporated area and heavily guarded by falling-down fences and No Trespassing signs pockmarked with BB gun divots and spray paint. At the beginning of each school year, the Hawthorne High principal worked an admonition into his welcome speech to students, telling them not to go to the Perc Ponds: They were dangerous, they were city property, trespassing was grounds for expulsion. But that speech came at the beginning of the school year after a summer full of partying along the Perc Pond banks, well after students had found their favorite spots and party grounds.

"Were there any clues inside?" Addie immediately felt dumb saying that, as though Lydia's killer would have left a calling card or murderous résumé tucked under the windshield wiper. "Or anything?"

Colton wagged his head. "It was empty. But the driver's side door was left open."

"Oh."

"The battery was dead so the police don't know if something happened with the car or—" he looked away, then bit his bottom lip, worrying it between crooked teeth.

"Or what?"

Colton jerked his head, and Addie followed him to a crook in the corridor that was less populated. "I'm not supposed to know this, you know…"

In addition to taking Addie's GapLakeLove site from pretty cool to CGI-amazing, Colton also dabbled in sporadic, mildly illegal hacking projects. Anything from looping in to police scanners to changing the occasional grade or two for desperate Hawthorne kids who had the money to pay. That kind of skill set gave Colton—big, loping, too-smart-for-his-own-good Colton—some street cred. He wasn't popular, but he wasn't shunned, either. Addie kind of admired it.

"I heard that someone actually called the abandoned car in. Said they saw headlights in the brush and that they had been there all night."

Addie shuddered. "Oh."

"Yeah, but by the time the cops got out there, there weren't any lights."

Addie's eyes flitted from Colton back toward Maya, dark ponytail disappearing through the masses of students. Usually she was up-to-the-moment refreshed on every police action in town— whether she wanted to be or not. Maya's parents thought the best way to keep her out of trouble was to detail the exact kind of trouble they dealt with—from meth heads to kidnapping—over family dinners. Addie loved it as fodder for her fanfic; Maya rolled her eyes and begged to move in with Addie.

"When they found the car," Colton was going on, "the key was still in the ignition, but the whole thing was dead."

Addie knew he was talking about a car, but Colton's use of the word *dead* sent another wave of shivers through her. She rubbed at the gooseflesh that pricked her arms. "Anything else?"

Colton's Adam's apple bobbed as he swallowed. "Her purse was in the car. Purse, keys, cell phone."

Now Addie was sweating. "Do you think she was pulled out of the car before...you know?"

"I overhead Maya's dad say that it looked like there was a struggle."

Addie's eyes widened. "You're sure it was Maya's dad?"

"I heard it on the scanner. His voice is pretty distinct with the accent and all."

Maya's father was originally from somewhere deep in the countryside. While he was all business on the job, the sharp, clipped words of the detective were softened somewhat by the slower drawl of the South.

"Maya didn't say anything?"

Addie shook her head. "I'm not sure she knew."

Colton just shook his head and kept talking. "He said that the dirt and brush around the car looked like it had been kicked up, and that there was some hair. But no blood or anything. The car being there gives them reason to believe she drowned."

She thought of her dream, of Lydia gone missing and turning up on the banks of Gap Lake. Then she remembered the water, Lydia Stevenson walking so peacefully in before dragging Addie down, the way the journalism room stank of water and mold.

"I think I'm going to be sick."

* * *

Addie made a beeline for the ladies' room, kicking open one of the stall doors before doubling over and heaving. Heat shot up the back of her neck and sweat dripped from her hairline and into her eyes. If Lydia's car was left behind—keys, cell phone, purse—and the police saw that there looked like there was a disturbance, then it was true: someone had attacked Lydia.

Life imitates art.

Addie couldn't get the waterlogged vision of Lydia out of her mind. She heaved again, then coughed, pressing her palms against the back of her neck and breathing deeply.

What the hell is going on?

"We need to do something. We need to have a march or a vigil for Lydia. Her family needs to know how much we loved her and will miss her." Addie stiffened as a girl walked into the bathroom, talking. "Her killer needs to know that we're going to find him."

"We shouldn't hold a vigil," someone answered the girl back. "We should just ask Spencer. He was the last one to see her. He probably knows exactly what happened."

"No, I don't believe Spencer did it. It's like that book, huh? The author makes it look like the boyfriend did it the whole time, but he didn't. He was being framed."

"How do you know that? The last book isn't even out yet."

Addie chanced a glance through the crack in the stall door, trying to discern who the two girls were. They were small and slight, looked like freshmen. One with a short blunt-cut bob was meticulously lining her eyes with another layer of coal while the other one was straightening and re-straightening an already perfect glossy black ponytail.

The ponytailed girl shrugged. "It's just a hunch I have."

NINETEEN

The sun was dipping behind the trees when Maya's car slowed to a stop in front of Bereman's Boutique.

"I can't believe you have a job."

Addie gathered up her backpack and eyed Maya. "You always say that."

"Your dad has money. Stupid money. You don't need to work."

"My *dad* has money," Addie specified. "I have a job."

The truth was, Addie took the job to get out of the house. The spending money was a bonus, but the fact that she didn't have to spend hours cooped up in a house where her father was perennially "on his way home" and where Louisa bumbled around doing mom things but not actually being a mom was the true benefit.

"Can you pick me up tonight?"

Maya shook her head, dug in the back seat, and plopped her big, striped Hot Dog on a Stick hat on her head. "Big corporate event. Lots of dogs, many sticks. Can't Daddy Warbucks get ya?"

Addie stiffened. She hated driving with her dad, even now that he drove with two hands clenched on the wheel, his eyes dead focused on the road, his breath smelling of old cigars and Altoids. He never drank anymore; he never sped, but Addie still had a hard time trusting him, had a hard time being behind the wheel with a man—even her own father—who had been so foreign to her that day at the market.

"Sure."

Addie pulled the door of the boutique open, inhaling the sweet smell of Bereman's rose-scented air freshener and new clothes.

"Addie!" Ella, the day manager, was the daughter of the owner and one of Addie's favorite people. She came around the register and engulfed Addie in a hug.

"I wasn't sure you'd make it in tonight after what happened."

Addie shifted her weight and Ella held her at arm's length. "You okay?"

She nodded. "Yeah…no. I mean, I…I don't know how to act. It was awful but I didn't really know Lydia and…" *Life goes on.* Maya's words came back, haunting, hanging on Addie's periphery.

Ella's eyes were soft but pained. "I just can't imagine what you must be going through. And that girl's parents…" She pressed her hands to her cheeks and shook her head so that her waist-length brown gray curls swirled, the streaks of gray catching in the fluorescent lights. "I can't believe people aren't more concerned."

Addie looked over her shoulder as though concerned citizens or killers would be lining the streets.

"Do you know if there have been any leads?"

Addie thought of Spencer, of the shocked, scared look on his face as he stood at his locker. She thought of R. J. Rosen. *Who really is R. J. Rosen?* "I don't know," she said, immediately busying herself tagging a stack of blue blouses. "I don't know who would do that."

As she tagged, she replayed that night over and over in her head. Lydia, crumpled.

Did you like my surprise?

Gap Lake.

She licked her lips, didn't look up from her task. "You know the Gap Lake books?"

"Of course I do," Ella said, draping a scarf around a mannequin. "If you're not reading them, you're talking about them."

"Do you think it's possible that…that someone may have wanted to make Lydia's murder sound like one from the book?"

Ella stopped fiddling with the scarf and looked at Addie. "Is that what Maya's dad is thinking?"

Addie shook her head. "No. I don't think so."

R. J. Rosen made his career selling mystery novels. He made his career putting pen to paper and committing murder in the pages of a book. This wasn't R. J. Rosen's work. No—Lydia's death was the work of someone who wanted to bring R. J. Rosen's work to life.

A copycat.

"I need to make a phone call," Addie said, dropping the heap of blouses. She went into the storeroom and dialed Maya's cell phone.

"Humiliation on a stick, this is Maya speaking."

"What if it's a copycat?" Addie said quickly.

"Qué?" Maya asked.

"I know it's dumb that I thought R. J. Rosen might be

responsible for Lydia's death. It's obviously just a coincidence." Addie pulled on her sweater but still shivered. "A really weird coincidence. But, what if the person who did this was copying the murder from the book?"

Maya let out a long sigh, and Addie couldn't quite tell if it was exasperation or consideration.

"You said what happened to Lydia looked like it came from a story R. J. Rosen sent you. How would anyone know about that?"

"And you said that I was being crazy. But what isn't crazy is the other stuff: a girl killed at school, the swampy stink. In the first book, Crystal Lanier went missing from the school when she was there at night. Yes, it turned out she was kidnapped and then drowned, but she was found facedown in the lake. Swampy smelling."

"Addie—"

"And in the book her car was found—"

"On the banks of Gap Lake."

"Kind of like the Perc Ponds where Lydia's car was found."

There was a long pause. "So you think some obsessed super-fan thought it would be some sort of homage to kill Lydia Gap Lake–style?"

Addie pinched her lip. "It's a theory."

"Addie, hon, I hate to break it to you, but the only Gap Lake superfan in town is you."

TWENTY

A *ping* from her cell phone pulled Addie out of a thankfully dreamless sleep. She rolled over, started to scroll before thinking. Her eyes widened when she saw who it was from. Addie thumbed open the message.

TheRealRJRosen:

> I'm a bit disappointed in you, Addie.
> I noticed you didn't post the story
> last night.

Addie's heart thumped. She licked her lips and started to type.

AddieGaines:

> I'm sorry. There's a lot going on here.
> I wasn't able to get around to it.

She counted the beats of her heart until the phone pinged again.

TheRealRJRosen:

You promised.

Addie chewed her thumbnail, breathing hard until the next message popped up.

TheRealRJRosen:

This is a very important launch for me. If it's not something you think you can do, please let me know and I'll have another blogger take your place.

Heat singed Addie's cheeks. This was her dream. This was R. J. Rosen writing to her, and she wasn't going to mess it up.

AddieGaines:

No, no, I'm super sorry. I'll post the story right now and be completely on top of it from now on. Thank you so much for giving me this chance—I promise, no more screwups!

Addie turned her phone off before R. J. Rosen could respond.

* * *

Addie padded down the stairs, the silence unnerving. Usually at that hour there were pots clanking, Louisa singing some funky mash-up of songs she didn't know the actual words to, and her father in front of the TV, furiously mashing the Volume button to drown out Louisa's sound track. But today it was almost silence, a thick haze of muffled sounds like everyone was trying to be quiet. When Addie reached the kitchen, that's exactly how it seemed. The TV was on but the volume way down. Louisa had three frying pans going on the stove, but even the bacon seemed reluctant to sizzle or pop.

"Hello?"

Addie's voice threw everything into hyper speed. Louisa turned and was manning her frying pans in a matter of seconds, flipping a pancake with one hand, shaking the bacon with the other.

"Everything okay here?"

Morton and Louisa both gave sharp, clipped head nods.

"Okay…"

Louisa turned, the smile on her face forced and overly bright. "Bacon and pancakes?"

Addie glanced down at the glistening bacon in the frying pan.

"Let me give you some."

Addie swallowed hard, nowhere near hungry, but she dutifully took the plate Louisa handed her and took her place at the kitchen table opposite her father. The newspaper was spread in front of him, a spray of crumbs across the NASDAQ index, but he wasn't reading. His eyes were on the television, on the anchorwoman stationed outside of Hawthorne High, her concerned voice a weird droning murmur with the volume turned down. He reached forward and clicked off the set.

"You're coming straight home after school today."

Addie blinked, poked at the too-crisp bacon on her plate. It immediately crumbled, submerged itself in a rainbow-y pool of grease. "What? Why?"

"Just do as you're told, Addie."

Addie carefully put down her knife and fork, wiped the grease from her fingertips. "Why?"

"Do I have to spell it out for you? One of your classmates is dead and they don't have any leads on who did it."

"They don't even know what happened, Dad."

Addie's father shook his head. "Addie, that girl was drowned."

If her father kept talking, Addie couldn't hear him. The kitchen seemed to wobble and go out of focus, and Addie's stomach clenched like a fist. "How do you know that?"

"It was in the paper this morning," Louisa supplied.

Addie tried to lick her lips, tried to form words and sentences, but her tongue felt enormous, leaden. "Can I see that?" she asked finally.

Louisa's eyes widened and Morton nodded slowly; Addie reached out for the paper and skimmed, passing over the normal rhetoric, the mention of Hawthorne High and the journalism department. Her breath caught when she saw what she was looking for:

"…*Preliminary autopsy reports say that seventeen-year-old Lydia Stevenson was most likely asphyxiated by drowning…*"

"We found her in the journalism room," she said, shaking her head incredulously.

"But her car was found out by the Percolation Ponds, yes?"

Addie licked her lips, gave Louisa a small nod.

"Honey, someone drowned this girl and then left her in a spot where she could easily be found."

Addie started to shake, the black words on the gray newsprint marching in front of her like ants, then scattering in a million directions.

She had been drowned.

Addie's dream came flashing back to her.

The smell of the journalism room.

Crystal Lanier had been drowned too.

"Don't you know life imitates art?"

Addie watched as her father methodically added cream and sugar to his coffee, then stirred: three in one direction, three in the other. Addie vaguely wondered if he had always done that, always been so meticulous.

"I won't take a chance on you."

Addie wanted to warm to her father. She wanted to swell with love and pride: her father didn't want anything happening to her! But it seemed like such an afterthought, such an add-on. He had drunk a bottle of bourbon and gotten behind the wheel. He had picked her up from school when he could hardly recognize her through the spirited haze.

And *now* he cared.

Addie ripped off a piece of pancake, chewed without really tasting it.

"Sure, Dad. Maya can get me home."

"Louisa will be here when you do."

She cut her eyes to Louisa, who immediately broke her gaze,

started polishing the already polished marble on the kitchen island. Louisa glanced up from her work, her eyes settling on Morton.

"I'm going to wait for Maya outside," she said.

It was unseasonably cold outside and Addie briefly considered going back into the house to grab her big jacket. But then she remembered it was draped across Maya's back seat because Maya had borrowed it, and as great a friend as Maya was, once she borrowed, she rarely returned. Instead, Addie pounded her hands against her arms and shifted from foot to foot, trying to work some feeling into her toes.

"What are you doing, Adds, chilling?" Colton was standing on his porch, smiling way too broadly for his horrible joke. Addie rolled her eyes, then narrowed them.

"Wow. As far as bad jokes go, that's, like, dad-level bad."

Colton mimed straightening his lapel, his smile still ear to ear. "I got a million of 'em."

"I wouldn't brag about that."

"Hey, you okay?" Colton asked.

Addie shook her head. "Did you hear about Lydia?"

Colton studied her. "I was there."

"No," Addie shook her head. "They said she was drowned. That someone drowned her and then put her in the journalism room."

His face paled. "Did they want us to find her?"

"I don't know. Who would do that? If you kill someone, don't you want to keep it hidden?"

Colton crossed his arms in front of his chest. "Well, the journalism room is new. It used to just be storage. Maybe they thought…" He shrugged. "Maybe they thought no one would find her for a while?"

They stood in silence for what seemed like an eon before Addie spoke. "So I saw Spencer over here the other day."

Colton brightened. "Why, Addie Gaines! You're a regular peeper! I mean, I have my heart set on being Mr. Maya Garcia, but I guess I could squeeze you in if you're so into me that you'll spy…"

Addie rolled her eyes. "We're next-door neighbors, Colt. I happened to be walking by one of my windows, and I saw you and Spencer. And it looked like Spencer was moving in."

Colton looked skeptical. "So I'm suppose to buy this 'just walking by the window' bull, huh? Okay, I guess."

"You're gross. So is Spencer setting up house with you or what?"

"No. I barely know the kid. He was dropping off shit for my mom."

"Spencer's a delivery boy?"

Colton shrugged. "His mom's my mom's pusher."

Addie gaped. "Your mom does drugs?"

"She does Tupperware. Or leggings. Or candles or whatever. Spencer's mom sells it, my mom buys it, and a couple of times a month ole Spence drops by and we make awkward conversation while my mom writes a check and I get a pair of buttery soft leggings." He kicked out a mammoth long leg.

"Nice."

"The guy's weird, but his scented candle stock is top notch. I could light a few if you're planning on peeping tonight…"

"You're so weird."

"Thank you. Hey, do you need a ride?"

Addie squinted down the long, serpentine road into Black Rock Hills Estates. She could see the huge wrought-iron gates yawning open, the specks of cars zipping by in the expressway just beyond. And then she saw Maya, the half-dead Accord sputtering and popping its way down the expressway, creeping through the gates.

"Nah, Maya's right there."

Colton's mouth opened slightly, a wash of uber-pink going over his ears and straight to his scalp. He stiffened and took a chest-heaving breath.

"I don't mean to sound callous about the whole Lydia thing and our new burgeoning love affair but…how do I look?"

"Like you always do."

He frowned. "Is that good?"

Addie offered him a benign half smile. "You look great, Colton."

Colton rubbed his hands together. "I love her, you know. Maybe I should just tell her? Like, just casually be all, 'Hey, Maya, I love you. I love you with the heat of a thousand burning suns.'"

Addie shielded her eyes with her hand. "That would be super casual. But I don't recommend it right now."

"You mean because of us?"

"There is no us, Colton. And maybe with Maya, you might want to be a little more subtle."

"Subtle, yeah." Colton nodded, then kicked up a heel, grabbing his ankle.

"Are you stretching? What exactly are you planning to do to

Maya? You know, she's my best friend, so it behooves me to look out for her."

He bobbled his head from side to side, cracking his neck, then dropped his foot. "I just want to be, you know, ready. And nice use of 'behooves,' by the way."

Addie shrugged.

"So you don't think now is the time to tell her?"

Addie didn't have the heart to tell Colton that Maya already knew he was in love with her. She had known since the first day she moved there, the first day she walked into the cafeteria and Colton bought her two plates of "welcome fries," then clumsily dumped them in her lap in a botched attempt at a grand gesture.

"You know what? I'd wait. At least until second period. Or prom. Or maybe even graduation, you know? Do it up real nice then."

Colton nodded, considering. "Graduation, huh? I could, like, sing to her when I'm walking to get my diploma."

"Yes, you could totally do that." Addie stood, seeing Maya's car creeping closer, already hearing the thump of the bass seeping from the windows. Maya's car might have been worth fifteen hundred bucks, but the stereo alone was worth twice that. She reasoned that she needed a top-notch stereo to keep her "sane" while she drove from one hellhole to the other: Hawthorne High, then her job at Hot Dog on a Stick. "Have you seen my uniform?" She had asked Addie once. "It's either a kicking stereo system or drugs, and you don't want to see me on drugs, do you, Addison?"

Colton yanked open his car door, a look of sheer terror striking across his face. "I probably shouldn't be here when she gets here, huh? I might do something stupid."

Addie tried not to laugh as Colton—six-foot, three-inch Colton—folded himself into the front seat of his car. He could only ever take two passengers with him since the driver's seat had to be pushed back clear against the passenger seat. Addie was certain that at least five and a half feet of Colton was long, skinny legs. Just as he backed out, Maya pulled up.

TWENTY-ONE

"Colton too afraid to talk to me?" Maya asked.

"You are terrifying."

"But only in the best possible way, right?"

Addie nodded. "Oh, yeah. Hey, do you have my jacket?"

Maya twisted herself and did an inelegant dive into the back seat-turned-closet. "This one or this one?" She held up two. "Or a sweatshirt?"

"How many of my clothes do you have in here, you little thief?"

"A, I always ask before I take and B, don't think of it as thieving. Think of this as your adjunct mobile closet."

Maya seemed immensely proud of herself. Addie groaned. "Is this my jacket? I don't even remember it."

"See? The benefits of me just keep coming. Everything old is new again. You're welcome. You got this when your dad went to Paris, I think."

Addie slipped into it, examined herself in the little makeup mirror. "Nice."

"And perfect for you because this one…" She pulled a purple

velvet, mid-thigh-length coat with a big fluffy collar that Addie wore all last year into her lap. "This one is becoming my statement piece."

"And is that statement 'I want to be Addison Gaines'?"

Maya pursed her lips, turned the key in the ignition until the car coughed back to life. "Maybe," she grumbled.

* * *

"It's a zoo out here," Maya said, once they arrived on campus. She slammed her car door and turned the lock.

Something like anxiety thrummed through Addie. It hurt to breathe and her heart was pounding in her chest. There were cops on campus, cops and reporters and the grief counselors who walked around with clipboards and drawn faces. Students milled around, formed circles, sat on benches with their heads in their hands or crying on each other's shoulders. The We love you Lydia posters had been picked apart by the night winds, the tape loosened and flapping in the breeze, Lydia's smiling picture rolling over itself.

Addie's stomach lurched.

"I have to get out of here."

She headed to the ladies' room, winding her way through news anchors giving their "countdown" pieces, past the grief counselors who offered her business cards or age-appropriate "comforting" taps on the shoulder.

Addie shrugged them off. "I just need to—"

"Hey, Addie!" It was Spencer, but still Addie didn't stop.

She made it into the ladies' room in time to double over, grip her knees, and pant.

"Oh God."

She thought of Lydia, of the smiling, cheerful girl she had seen on Spencer's arm. She thought of the girl she had seen in that very bathroom, the U-shaped bruise forming on her lower arm.

What exactly happened to Lydia Stevenson?

None of that could block out R. J. Rosen's latest missive, his quick detail of a scene from the next book:

The stench of blood was overwhelming. Metal mixed with raw meat and something else—alcohol? Bleach? Was he trying to clean up?

Jordan's stomach clenched, bile itching at the back of her throat. She was moving slowly, painfully slow but she had to. Whatever came through the needle, was in the plunger that he shoved into her neck, was wearing off but still strong enough to make her every move an arduous effort, a thousand times harder than it should have been. She picked carefully through the darkness, through the angles and planes of the strange house. House? Was it a house? Could it be? A house was a warm comfort, a place to run to—not a place to run from. Jordan's foot, shuffling, dragging, hit something solid, something warm. There was a soft groan. Everything inside her seized up.

Don't look down.

Her bare foot touched something…something warm, something wet. Blood.

Was that a sigh?

Vaulting back to high school. A classroom. Nondescript. A lecture.

"A body will sigh, wheeze, even gasp after death."

After death?

Jordan could feel eyes on her. She was prey, plain and simple, and someone was watching her in this macabre scene. She heard the voice next, dull and grating as a serrated blade.

"You should run," it said.

TWENTY-TWO

Addie's arrow hovered over the Post button. She steadied herself, then clicked. She was thrilled that R. J. Rosen didn't hold her non-post against her. With the swipe of a finger, Rosen's story zoomed through cyberspace and Addie's GapLakeLove readers were going to flip.

It didn't take long for the first message to hit.

CRYSTALFAN321: OMG.

Then, two more—

VALERIE4: Love this!
SEEULTR: Sooooooo creepy!

She plopped onto her bed, pulling her laptop onto her crossed legs. Her stomach continued its wild flutter, her shoulders breaking out in a damp sweat. R. J. Rosen was emailing her! It was almost like she was on a date with her idol—if only she knew what he looked like…

Thanks so much for the post, Addie! My publicity
team is thrilled! Your post has tons of comments,
and the page hit counter is going through the roof!

Addie fanned herself, glancing at the page counter at the
bottom of her site. The new story already showed reads in the high
hundreds, and the comments kept coming. She was beaming.

Now, the next part of the launch comes tomorrow
and there's a huge surprise in it for you too! I hope
you'll be as excited as I am.

Addie laid her fingers over her keys. "I love it!!!!" she started writing,
before erasing the myriad of exclamation points. She didn't want to
seem like a rabid superfan or even a little girl. She wanted R. J. Rosen
to think of her as his colleague, maybe even one day his equal.

"That sounds spectacular," she spoke as she wrote. "Looking
forward to it."

"Knock, knock."

Addie's father stood in her doorway, doing that precursory
knock thing that parents do before walking into your room
without being asked. He shot Addie a warm smile and sat down at
her desk chair, sighing.

"You getting ready for bed?"

"Yeah, Dad, in a minute."

"You know I was thinking that maybe I could take you out
driving this weekend."

Addie shifted on her bed. She didn't want to look at her father, especially the way he was staring at her like she was some animal in a zoo, like he was waiting for her to pounce.

"I'm actually working at the boutique this weekend. All weekend," she clarified, keeping her eyes on her screen.

"Addie—"

"Sorry, Dad, but you always say that work is a priority."

He nodded, sucking in a long breath and looking away. "What are you working on?"

Addie was too excited, too proud to lie. "A story. I just posted this on my site. Look at the comments!"

She handed over her laptop. Her dad scanned the comments and nodded appreciatively. "Lots of people seem to really like what you do here, Adds."

He scrolled up, his eyes darting across the screen as he read. Even though it was R. J. Rosen's work, not her own, Addie could feel her pulse ratchet up and the hum of nerves like bees in her brain. Would he like it? Would they actually have something in common—something besides that terrible night?

"Well," Addie asked when he looked up from the screen. "What do you think?"

Mr. Gaines scratched at his chin, his eyes flitting back to the screen. "I think you should delete it."

Addie gaped. "What?"

"It's absolutely disrespectful, Addison. A girl in your class is dead and you post this murder story on your website? Delete it."

"No, Dad, I can't—it's fiction anyway."

He handed her the laptop. "Delete it."

"I can't. I won't."

He shook his head and stood up, opened his mouth to say something and then thought better of it.

"Dad, it's just fiction and my readers are from all over the country. Hardly anyone in my school even knows that I'm the one who runs this site so no one is going to…to…" she thought of Lydia, laughing, head thrown back, and then the empty seat when Lydia sat in her AP bio class. She thought of the posters that had gone up, the candles, the memorial. Was she really a terrible person?

"No one is going to think that this story has anything to do with Lydia Stevenson," she said.

Right?

TWENTY-THREE

Addie handed the cashier her money and took her latte when Colton came barreling up behind her.

"Have you seen your blog yet?"

"What? No, why? What's going on?" Addie started to wrestle her laptop out of her bag while Colton bounded from foot to foot behind her.

"Everyone is talking about it! You must have posted something good."

Maya edged in between Colton and Addie. "Are you serious? Adds, you're famous!"

"I'm not," Addie said, "R. J. Rosen is."

Colton chimed in. "Once you posted that first story—and oh my God, I have to say, I don't read that stuff normally but—"

"Because then you can't sleep at night?" Maya said with an enormous mock frown and big, batting eyelashes.

"Yeah, I have trouble sleeping at night. Want to come and keep me company?" Colton arched an eyebrow, and Maya stuck her tongue out at him.

"Wait, what are you guys talking about?" Addie wanted to know. "I didn't post a new story. I posted R. J. Rosen's story—"

"Oh my God."

Addie's laptop was open, the GapLakeLove site immediately popping up and populating the screen.

"Did you do that? Addie, that's horrible." Maya's eyes darkened and she shook her head, her dark hair cascading over her shoulders. "How could you do that?"

Colton was pale. He swallowed hard, his Adam's apple bobbing. "Addie?"

Addie looked at her screen and her stomach turned.

Her beautiful banner was gone. The pretty logo that she and Colton had worked so hard on was anemic looking, drowned out by a slash-style logo done in blood red: LIFE IMITATES ART. Underneath were pictures of Lydia. It seemed like there were hundreds of them, exploding on the screen one after another: Lydia on the debate team. Lydia as homecoming princess. Lydia grinning in the quad. One by one the pictures popped up with dizzying fury and one by one they were scratched out by the blood red slasher font.

Lydia in her car on the day that she died.

Lydia from behind a clutch of bushes on the way to the journalism building.

Lydia looking over her shoulder, eyes wide, lips pulled into a terrified grimace.

And Lydia, in the journalism room, head bowed, body crumpled at the desk.

Addie slammed the laptop shut. She wanted to speak, to scream, to protest, but she was terrified that if she opened her mouth, she would throw up. The tears started immediately. "I didn't do this. You guys have to believe me. I didn't...I wouldn't."

Colton and Maya were staring at her, silent.

"Say something! Maya, you know I wouldn't."

The tears were pouring over Maya's cheeks, and she clapped a hand over her mouth.

Colton frowned. "Addie, who had access to your computer?"

"What? Nobody. It's been in my backpack since I got home from school yesterday."

"What about passwords? Someone could have accessed the site."

"No," Addie shook her head, used the back of her hand to wipe at her eyes. "No, only you and me. We have to get this off there, Colton. We have to get this off there right now. People are seeing this. People are hitting the site and they're going to think that we did this, that we think this is okay. It's not, it's not!" Addie was crying hard, big racking sobs that hurt her rib cage. Maya immediately snatched her in a hug.

"We'll get rid of it right now. Right now. Shut it down, Colton. Shut it down, right now."

Colton already had the laptop open, the flashes from Lydia's pictures casting a sickly glow over his face. His fingers flew over the keyboard, and he went from a gentle maneuver to stabbing at the keys. "I can't."

"What do you mean, 'you can't'? Shut it down, Colton. You don't have to fix it, just shut the goddamn thing down."

"Whoever did this changed all the passwords. The site is locked, Addie. I can't—we can't do anything."

Addie gaped. "No, you're wrong." She shoved Colton from his desk chair and started pounding keys randomly. "The password is Declan Levy. I know it is. I'm sure of it. Colton, it's not working. Why isn't it working?"

Each time she typed, the screen froze, then vibrated. A red box with a black skull and crossbones shot across the screen, the words *PASSWORD DENIED* emblazoned in front. "I don't understand."

Colton leaned forward and flicked the Power button, the offending screen going mercifully black and silent.

"Did you do it?" Maya asked quietly.

Colton's jaw was set hard, his eyes downcast. "I just turned off the computer. I'm sorry, Addie, I don't know what happened."

"Can you…can you find out who hacked it?"

"There's nothing there. I looked at the source files, the server codes…everything I could find."

"And?" Addie asked.

Colton just shrugged. "I know computers pretty well but whoever did this"—he held up his hands—"knows way more than I do. I'm so sorry, Addie."

A fresh wave of tears broke over Addie and her shoulders slumped. "People are going to think I'm responsible for this. They're going to think I'm some sort of horrible person who—"

"No." Maya put her hands on Addie's shoulders, stared her full in the face. "No one is going to believe for a minute that you had anything to do with this."

Addie swallowed, her stomach hollow. "I don't know why someone would do this to me. To Lydia."

Maya gathered her best friend in a hug and a beat later, Colton's long arms snaked around both girls. "We're really screwed right now, you guys. Really freaking screwed," Colton said.

"We're going to tell my parents." Maya said definitively.

"As parents, or as police?" Colton wanted to know.

"As police," Maya said, "and no, I don't care what R. J. Rosen thinks, Addie."

Addie shrugged. "I wasn't going to say anything about R. J." She sucked in a breath. "This is too much. This isn't R. J. Rosen. This is someone who…" A sob seized in her throat. "Who wants to hurt us."

TWENTY-FOUR

Addie slid her laptop into her bag. She, Colton, and Maya stood up and walked in a silent line out of the coffee shop. Addie felt like a trapped rat, like everyone was already staring her down, sure she was guilty. Humiliation and angst gnawed at her, sending a sticky heat all over her body.

"Hey, isn't that your housekeeper?"

Addie squinted toward where Colton was pointing. It was Louisa, in a maroon car Addie didn't recognize, pulling out of the spot next to Maya's ancient Accord.

"She drinks coffee, so what?" Maya said. "We need to do this."

Addie watched Louisa flip gears and click on her blinker before easing out into the intersection. She was sure Louisa's eyes caught hers when they flicked up at the rearview mirror but she made no motion to acknowledge Addie.

Maybe she saw the blog, Addie thought miserably. *She probably thinks I'm a psycho killer too.*

"Do you guys want me to drive you?" Colton asked.

Addie shook her head. "You don't need to come with, Colton."

She patted the laptop in her bag. "I've got everything I need, I guess."

Maya squeezed Addie's arm. "It's going to be okay. My parents will know what to do. They're going to nab this jerk and then we'll all go to Hawaii." She shot Addie a weak smile.

"Sure. Let's just get this over with."

Addie belted herself into the passenger seat of Maya's car, still gripping her bag and her laptop. They watched Colton belt himself into his car, give a solemn wave, and pull into traffic.

"You okay?"

Addie nodded. "Let's just do this."

"It's really going to be okay, you know?"

Addie swallowed the sob in her throat. She wanted to believe her best friend. She wanted to believe this story could have a happy ending, but it seemed like it was never going to end.

* * *

As soon as they got to the station and were ushered into an interrogation room, Addie sat and pulled her laptop out of her bag, her dog-eared copy of *Murder at Gap Lake* coming out with it. She rolled her thumb over the raised lettering of the title, of the two-inch embossed letters of R. J. Rosen's name.

"Dad, someone crashed Addie's blog site."

"Girls, we're in the middle of an investigation—"

"They posted pictures of Lydia all over my blog, Detective Garcia. Whoever did this posted pictures of Lydia on the day that she died."

The color drained from Detective Garcia's face. "Show me."

Addie swallowed hard and pulled out her laptop, clicking on her site. GapLakeLove populated the screen.

The regular blog.

The pictures of Lydia were gone, the horrible slashes of color and the screaming, *Life imitates art* text was gone.

Addie felt like she had been punched in the stomach.

"I don't think I understand," Detective Garcia said.

Addie pulled out her own phone, jumped to the site there. The lake shimmered behind the GapLakeLove logo. In the center was R. J. Rosen's newest story. No Lydia. Just Addie's site.

"Girls, I really don't have time—"

"No," Addie shook her head, her mind spastically pinballing. Who had ruined her site in the first place—and who had fixed it? Colton had said that all the passwords were changed and locked.

What was going on?

She blinked up at the detective. "Someone hijacked my website. They...they put up all these horrible pictures, pictures of Lydia Stevenson, but it wasn't me, I swear."

"It's true, Dad, I saw it. I saw the pictures on her blog."

"But it's all fixed now?" Detective Garcia didn't hide the skepticism in his voice.

"It was there," was all Addie could say.

"And who are you thinking is responsible for this?"

Addie shook her head. "I don't know who hacked my site. I don't know who's doing all this."

R. J. Rosen.

No.

Someone pretending to be R. J. Rosen hacked her site. It had to be. He was playing some sort of sick cat-and-mouse game, he was framing her, he was—

Maya pumped her head. "This deranged author had been emailing Addie—"

Addie shook her head. "Someone wants me to believe it's R. J. Rosen. Someone wants this story to be real."

The detective looked from Maya to Addie, eyes hard. "I really don't have time for your stories today."

* * *

Days later, Lydia's death was still all over the news. Every station covered it, even the satellite ones and the ones out of other states. Hawthorne High was famous, and it made Addie sick to her stomach. They flashed pictures of Lydia too, her senior portrait where she was grinning with narrowed eyes.

Just like Crystal Lanier.

Addie channel surfed, looking for anything other than the news—hoping for a train of reruns or the merciful drone of an infomercial—before the cover of *Murder at Gap Lake* flashed on-screen. A woman with a blond bouffant and a severe red suit with enormous shoulder pads was bobbing her head emphatically. Addie turned up the sound.

"…It's not just movies and video games anymore, or rap music with its explicit lyrics. Kids are being bombarded with messages from their peers, the internet and even in writing. This book is in the Gap Lake mystery series and it seems harmless enough.

It's a mystery about two teens who go missing. One turns up dead and the other—well, the"—and here the woman made air quotes—"mysterious author R. J. Rosen wants us to wait and see. But this book is atrocious. Basically an A-B-C of how to commit murder. Just fiction you say? Not influencing our children? Just this week there was a murder in the small town of Crescent City. A teenager—very pretty, very popular, just like the main character in this book—turns up dead. Her car was found at the banks of a local pond. And I read to you—"

The woman slid a pair of glasses down her nose, opened up the Gap Lake book to a yellow Post-it note, and began reading.

"They've found Crystal's car. It was at Gap Lake, in the lower lot—that's why it took so long to find. It was unlocked; the keys were in the ignition but the car was completely out of gas. Initially, the police thought that Crystal must have hit empty, then set out to walk to get gas. But her purse was on the passenger seat. Purse with wallet inside. No cell phone, though. They still hadn't recovered that."

The woman looked up, narrowed her eyes at the camera, and cleared her throat. "Again, that was a direct quote from the Gap Lake book that has taken the publishing world by storm. Kids are gobbling this book up. Now let me read you something else."

The woman fumbled with something, deliberately holding it off camera.

"Police found Lydia Stevenson's car parked at the Percolation Ponds located behind Hawthorne High School. An anonymous call reported an abandoned car with the lights left on. Once the police arrived, they found Stevenson's car with a dead battery. Keys were still in the ignition, and both Stevenson's cell phone and purse were left in the car." Here the woman looked up, pausing dramatically. "I'm not reading from R. J. Rosen's book. I'm not reading from another author's book. I'm reading from the Crescent City police report."

Another awkward pause as though the viewing audience would somehow respond with audible shock and horror.

"Now, Lydia Stevenson is dead and the circumstances of her death seem eerily reminiscent of this book. Is it a work of fiction? Or a guidebook for murder?"

Addie clicked off the television, an odd sense of cold engulfing her. Gap Lake was a mystery series. It was well written, sure—but a "guidebook for murder"? She should have laughed. She should have shrugged the whole thing off, but the similarities were uncanny and in the back of her head, she was thinking the same thing.

And then there was her website.

But who—and why?

Addie found herself pacing, worrying her bottom lip until it was raw. A fan? Could someone actually be crazy enough to believe that killing someone—killing a *real person*—would prove that they were the biggest fan of Gap Lake or R. J. Rosen? She shook her head. That seemed silly. But still she had read internet posts and news stories about kids killing for less—attempting murder to pay homage to internet memes or urban legends.

But to a book—or an author?

Then there was R. J. Rosen.

An anomaly. A mystery himself.

Or a killer.

She dialed Maya. "Did you see—"

"That whacked-out news report? Yes."

Addie paced. "Do your parents think it could be true?" She shivered just saying it, pulling her sweater tighter around her and staring out the windows. They overlooked the backyard with the glowing pool, and yellow light swathed the trunks of the palm trees. Normally, the backyard was a tropical oasis, but tonight everything took on an eerie glow.

Maya sucked in a breath. "Addie, I have to tell you something."

TWENTY-FIVE

Just then the doorbell rang.

"I've got to call you back, Mys. Someone's at the door."

"Yeah, that's what I wanted to—"

"Who is it?"

"Crescent City police."

Addie dropped the phone.

The police?

She rolled up on her tiptoes and peered through the peephole.

The police were at her door.

Two officers in full uniform.

Immediately, Addie's thoughts turned to Lydia, to everything in the news. Maybe they were coming to tell her that her father had been killed. Addie's heart was hammering like a fire bell, sweat dripping down her spine.

Another knock. This one was fiercer. "Ma'am?"

Addie pulled open the door a half inch. She wasn't sure what she was expecting. Lights. Sirens. Gunfire. But the two officers just smiled at her before the first one, a woman with close-cropped hair, spoke.

"Addison Gaines?"

Addie nodded, her mouth full of sand.

"I'm Officer Chadwick and you might remember Officer Olson. Is your father home?"

Addie's heart slammed against her rib cage.

This wasn't happening. This couldn't be happening.

Not again.

The kitchen light was off, but she could see him in there, her father, sitting at the table in the dark. She could smell the heady steam of his too-strong coffee and when she flicked on the light, he cringed.

"Turn it off, please." His voice was gruff, odd sounding, and she snapped the light back off immediately—more out of shock than anything else.

"Are you okay, Dad?"

"Your aunt Katie will be picking you up any minute. Can you throw a few things in a bag for me?"

"Am I going to stay with Auntie?"

"Just for tonight."

Addie shifted her weight. "But it's a school night."

She could see her father's hands circle the mug as he brought it to his mouth, took a long, slow sip. "Just do this for me, okay, sweets?"

Addie nodded and climbed the stairs. By the time she reached her room and shoved her toothbrush and a change of clothes in her backpack, she was crying. She didn't know why. Downstairs, the kitchen lights were still off, but her father was in the foyer now, his face drawn and illuminated by the police car's flashing blue light.

"Morton Gaines? You're being charged with leaving the scene of an accident."

Addie saw the officer's hands, the silver flash from the handcuffs he offered. And the farmer's market flashed in front of her eyes. It was embarrassing but no one was hurt except a table of cabbages. She remembered her father stumbling out of the car, curling a fat stack of bills into a man's hands. Then they went home and ate pizza.

Nothing else happened.

"I'm turning myself in," her father had said in that same gravelly voice. "My lawyer said there would be no cuffs."

"Addison?" The officer tried again.

Addison's saliva tasted sour, and though she tried to form words, to press them over her teeth and out of her mouth, she couldn't. All she could do was shake her head.

"Officer Olson and I would like to ask you a few questions, but we really can't do that without your father present. You're not in any trouble. I want you to know that."

Addie heard the sounds, but couldn't put value to them. She shook her head dumbly. "Wait, what? What is this about?"

"We'd like to talk to you about Lydia Stevenson. Completely off the record, of course."

She nodded, somehow still feeling that this was wrong. "I don't really know her."

"And Spencer Cohen?"

Heat zinged across Addie's body. She shifted her weight, feeling ice shoot through her veins. "We're just friends."

"Can you tell us your impression of him?"

Addie shrugged her shoulders. "He's nice, I guess."

"And what can you tell us about GapLakeLove? What can you tell us about that site, Addison?" Olson smiled kindly but fireworks exploded behind Addie's eyes. She wanted to slam the door and run. She wanted to slam the door, run, and forget about Lydia and Spencer and Gap Lake and, most of all, R. J. Rosen.

"Am I in trouble?" Her voice was a soft, shaky whisper that seemed to embolden Officer Olson's smile. Addie thought she meant it to be comforting, but there was a hint of menace to it that set Addie's teeth on edge.

"Trouble? No. Just asking some questions, trying to tie up some loose ends."

She had told the police.

And no one believed her.

Addie cleared her throat, then winced when the glare of headlights washed over her, sending a wave of black dots in front of her eyes. Her father pulled into the driveway at a dizzying speed, parking askew, hopped out of the car, and came charging toward the house.

"Addison! Addison, are you okay? Officers, what is going on here?"

Mr. Gaines engulfed his daughter in a hug that Addie found overly protective and awkward, but she was glad he was there.

"Nothing, Dad, they just wanted to talk."

Addie saw the color raise in her dad's cheeks, the tightening of his jaw. "Were you questioning my daughter?"

"Mr. Gaines, we—"

"Because I'd hate to think that the Crescent City Police Department was doing something untoward—interviewing a minor without the benefit of her parent present." His voice was a baritone that Addie recognized from calls that ended with a phone slam, or a slew of words she wasn't allowed to repeat in the house, and heat itched across her scalp.

"We were simply asking some informal questions, but now that you're here, if you'll allow it, we could go on the record. Addison, where were you at 4:00 p.m. on the night Lydia Stevens went missing?"

Addie felt the color drain from her face. "Am I a suspect?"

"Honey, you don't have to answer that. Officers, I did not give you permission to interrogate my daughter."

Addie pushed in front of her father's outstretched arm. "Am I a suspect? I was in school, and then Maya and I went to Starbucks. That's it. I didn't…I found her."

"Addison!"

"Dad, I want to answer them. I have nothing to hide. I had nothing to do with this, and the sooner they know that, the sooner they can find out who really killed Lydia." Addie didn't know where the speech, where the little bit of courage, was coming from, but she couldn't stop talking. "Please, Dad, I just want to get this over with."

Officer Chadwick scratched the back of her head. "We think it might be a good idea to shut down your website."

"My blog?"

"You post fan fiction there, right? Fan theories, that kind of thing?"

Addie nodded, deeply aware of her father's eyes firmly on her. "But it's not big deal."

"You posted a pretty detailed murder scene, did you not?"

"It was just…" Addie's mouth was dry. "Fiction. A story."

"Addison?" There was something in her father's eyes that stabbed at Addie's heart.

"I just wrote a piece of a story where a girl from Gap Lake High was murdered." She shook her head, tears pricking her eyes. "It was ages ago."

"And you posted a story in the school newspaper as well about"—Officer Olson flipped back in her notebook—"a popular girl who was lured by the school's 'nice girl,' who drowned her, did you not?"

Morton Gaines's eyes were wide, his lips pressed together hard.

"How did you know about that? I post anonymously."

"Lady A? We talked to the journalism teacher."

"They're just stories."

Addie could see her father swallow hard, his Adam's apple doing a slow bob. "Are you accusing my daughter of murder because she has a vivid imagination?"

Officer Olson shook her head and Chadwick stepped forward, a tight smile on her lips. "We're just asking some questions, sir."

"Well then, I think you're done."

Olson and Chadwick shared another glance, this one less obvious. Something in Addie's chest tightened and she shifted her weight. "Um, I really should get inside and do my homework."

She expected Olson or Chadwick to tell her no, that they weren't finished. She expected them to pin her with a glare or worse yet, slap handcuffs on her wrists and drag her to jail.

"No problem." Officer Olson reached into her pocket and handed Addie a business card that her father snatched away. "If you think of anything, please don't hesitate to call us." She offered a dazzling smile that send a chill down Addie's spine.

Addie may have watched the officers get back in their car and drive away. She couldn't remember. Her head was buzzing, her lips numb as she trudged to the dining room table and sat down. Her father sat across from her and knitted his hands in front of him.

"Why do you write those stories, Addison?"

Addie gaped. "Do you think I had something to do with Lydia's murder because of my stories?"

He cocked his head, a small puff of air escaping his lips. "That's a far stretch, Addison."

"Is it? The police don't seem to think so."

"The police are just trying to scare you."

Addie laid her head on the table. "It worked."

"The stories?"

"They're just for fun, Dad. They don't mean anything." He didn't answer and Addie pressed on. "I'm not depressed or obsessed with death or anything, if that's what you're thinking. I like to write stories. I like to write and read stories where people die because they're scary and sometimes it's fun to be scared when you're in control, you know?"

But she was definitely not in control now.

"Cut out the site and stop with the stories. Right now, they're just in bad taste."

"Dad—"

"Just do it, Addie." He stood up and turned his back on her. Conversation effectively over.

TWENTY-SIX

Maya was blowing up Addie's phone. She had called three times when Addie and her father were talking to the police, and twice since then. Finally, Addie picked up.

"My God, I thought you were dead in some ditch somewhere."

Addie didn't answer.

"I'm sorry, that came out way wrong. Are you okay?"

"The police were here."

There was a pause on Maya's end of the phone, and Addie could picture her best friend pinching her upper lip. "I know. I heard my dad on the phone. Is everything okay?"

"Does your dad think I had something to do with this?"

"No. No way. Of course not. I don't think so. Why?"

"The police know about GapLakeLove and the fanfic."

Maya was silent again and then, "So?"

"So I think they think that I could be a murderer because I wrote them."

"That's the stupidest thing I've ever heard. First of all, how do they even know it's you? You go by Lady A. Not the most original *nom de* plum—"

"*Plume.*"

"Whatever. Not the most original one of those ever, but still."

"Mr. Moreau told them."

"But why you? Why not some other rabid fan or, like, R. J. Rosen himself?"

"They probably don't even know who R. J. Rosen is. No one does. And he doesn't even live around here."

Does he?

Heat pricked out all over Addison, beating down the back of her neck. She was exposed; she felt eyes on her. "I don't know anything about R. J. Rosen."

"No one does."

"No, but I really don't. I…I don't even think the person emailing me is R. J. Rosen. I think it's a copycat."

Maya's voice was flat. "He emails you. Send him a questionnaire. Oh, shit."

"What?"

"What if R. J. Rosen isn't as much of a mystery as we think?"

Addie scratched her forehead. "I'm listening."

"What if he's someone we know, Adds? Someone we see every day even."

"Like who?"

"Mr. Moreau."

Addie snorted. "Mr. Moreau? Seriously?"

"Lot's of people live double lives, Addie."

"Yeah, but like a mild-mannered nursery school teacher slash internet porn star, not a multimillion-book-selling author slash teacher who gets off on catching prepositional phrases."

"Just think about it. It kind of lines up. He kills Lydia Stevensen for some sick and twisted bookish reason or cuz, you know, teachers go off the deep end. Or because he needed more stuff for his plot or whatever."

"Get on with it."

"He kills her, then when the police are closing in, he throws them a perfect suspect: his prize student, who just happens to write gnarly, death-filled fan fiction."

"I'm not his prize student."

Maya sighed. "Big picture, Addie."

Addie gnawed on Maya's theory. "I don't know. That just seems really weird. And far-fetched. And ridiculous."

"But you didn't say implausible."

"Hang up, Maya."

Addie changed into her pajamas and scrubbed her face, trying to wash off the debris of the day—of the week. Lydia, the police at her door, Maya's crazy Mr. Moreau theory, and shutting down her blog. It was all too much for her, a humming cacophony at the base of her spine making her head pound and her eye twitch. She wanted to brush the whole thing off and go to bed. Her phone pinged, the tone the sound of a fat rock dropping into a lake.

Someone had sent her an email through her blog site.

Addie's heart thudded in her throat. It was cold in her bedroom, the breeze outside lifting the curtains, but she was sweating. She slid her thumb over the alert, staring at it a full minute, mouth dry, before reading. A message from R. J. Rosen was the first on her list.

SUBJECT: Cover reveal

Addie clicked on the message even as her stomach dropped.

Hi Addie—

Attached please find a preview of the cover of the newest Gap Lake book! I hope you like it...

Addie licked her lips and hit the download button, her stomach turning somersaults. She was going to get to see the new Gap Lake cover! She couldn't believe her luck.

Then she couldn't believe her eyes.

The cover image was a photograph, barely tinged with color.

A blond, crumpled over a desk. Hair dripping. Bare feet covered in mud.

"No."

Addie recognized the room. She recognized the girl on the desk. She recognized the girl looking on, terrified.

It was her.

"What? This can't be—no!"

Maya was in the picture too, eyes wide, cell phone by her side.

LIFE IMITATES ART was scrawled across the top of the photograph.

A new message popped up on Addie's screen: TheRealRJRosen would like to talk. Are you available?

Addie's cursor hovered over the Decline box. But she accepted.

TheRealRJRosen:

Hello, Addie.

AddieGaines:

What the hell was that? That's not a cover, that's a picture. Where the hell did you get it? Who are you????
Is this some fucking joke???

TheRealRJRosen:

Are you laughing?

Addie sucked in a breath so sharp she thought it would pierce her lungs and waited, her pulse ratcheting up. The wind outside grew, rattling her open windows and snatching the curtains. She got up and slammed the window shut, glancing down into Colton's room. It was empty and dark, only the ominous glow from his computer visible. There was a ping from her machine.

AddieGaines:

No. This is horrible. You're horrible.
I'm not doing anything for you
anymore. Who even are you???

TheRealRJRosen:

You promised.

Something heavy and dark settled in Addie's gut. Her saliva soured and the words wobbled in front of her eyes. She was crying. A girl had died, she was crying, and this asshole was trying to make her feel guilty.

AddieGaines:

I'm done.

TheRealRJRosen:

We had a deal. You need to follow through. Follow-through is important. Don't you know that, Addison? Follow-through means everything.

Anger surged through her.

AddieGaines:

I said I'm done.

TheRealRJRosen:

I decide when we're done.

AddieGaines:

> I'm not posting that cover. It's
> horrible.

TheRealRJRosen:

> This cover?

Suddenly, Addie's screen exploded as file after file opened. They were all basically the same, all artwork and text from the *Life Imitates Art* cover, but each one was slightly nuanced—a different color, a different angle.

AddieGaines:

> I'm not talking to you anymore.

All the covers disappeared from her screen and Addie stared at the throbbing cursor. A pause that lasted an eternity. Then:

TheRealRJRosen:

> We don't have to talk. Post or else.

AddieGaines:

> Or else what?

TheRealRJRosen:

> :)

AddieGaines:

NO. I'm done.

TheRealRJRosen:

We're just getting started.

Addie gritted her teeth, the anger like a white-hot flame in her gut.

AddieGaines:

No. We're done. I'm done. Stop talking to me.

TheRealRJRosen:

Can't. The story is just getting good.

Addie slammed shut her laptop and shoved it under the bed. She was shaking, mad and terrified. Who was this person and why wouldn't he leave her alone? She jumped off the bed, pacing, pulling on her hair.

She would call the police.

She would call the police and the police would—what? They already suspected her of murder. Suddenly, her insides turned to jelly. She sunk down on the carpet and pulled her knees to her chest, shaking so hard her teeth were chattering. She was a suspect in a murder case because she wrote like her favorite author.

The story is just getting good.

Bile itched at the back of her throat. It was like a sick book.

Her life—her normal, boring life—was like a Gap Lake Mystery. She was being stalked by a madman, a girl was dead, and...what was next?

TWENTY-SEVEN

Addie wasn't sure how she slept. She knew she did, because she woke up in her bed, covers to her chin. She was still fully dressed and every inch of her body ached. Her head throbbed and her eyes were caked with goo that let her know that she had cried herself to sleep. She didn't want to think about what had happened, didn't want to think about R. J. Rosen or GapLakeLove or the fact that the police—*the police*—had come to her house and nearly accused her of murder.

No, Addie tried to correct herself, tried to console herself, they were just asking questions. She tried to steel herself, tried to breathe deeply, but dread held her down, settling on her chest like a two-ton weight.

"Addie, honey, you up?" He father poked his head through her door with a lopsided grin. "Louisa is downstairs. She made French toast."

Addie sniffed at the air. It was heady with cinnamon and vanilla, and she could hear the faint sound of a sizzling pan, of Louisa humming something as she flipped. "I don't feel so well, Dad."

The smile on Morton Gaines's face slipped and he stepped into Addie's room, pressing a cool palm against her forehead. "You okay, sweet cakes?"

Addie's stomach roiled and she rolled to one side, pressing her palms against her eyes. "Don't call me sweet cakes when I feel this barfy. Okay, Dad?"

"You could stay home. You could stay here today with Louisa, but you are going to have to go back to school eventually. And it's not like you did anything wrong."

Addie wanted to shrink down deeper into the covers. She wanted to clench her eyes closed and fall asleep, to drift off and wake up years from now when all of this was a distant memory, when Lydia Stevenson's real killer would be caught and no one would remember Addie's name—or Spencer's.

"I know that," she said in a low, strained voice.

"I should have stepped in the second I saw the police on our front porch."

Addie flashed back to Officers Chadwick and Olson. They were actually decent. Then she thought back to Maya's dad and the way he looked her up and down for the first time ever, like he was scrutinizing her, like he was sizing her up against the criminals he usually dealt with. Against the *murderers* he usually dealt with.

"No one believes you have anything to do with this, Addie."

"They want me to shut down my blog. You want me to shut it down."

Morton Gaines blinked. "I do. It's in bad taste, honey, especially now. How do you think it looks?"

Addie pushed herself to sitting. "What does it matter how it looks if I didn't have anything to do with Lydia's murder?"

"Kids could read it, get ideas…"

"Are you kidding? Do you really think that happens? Some kid reads some fan fiction and goes out and murders someone?"

Her father patted the covers softly. "Addie, calm down. I'm just telling you—how things look shouldn't be an issue and in a perfect world they wouldn't. But here we are."

"What does that even mean?"

"It means you're going to shut it down."

"So that's it?"

"Yes." Her father was on his feet so fast the bed wobbled. He clapped once, then smiled. "So how about that French toast?"

Addie wanted to force a smile. She wanted to believe that dropping the blog would make everything okay, but it didn't. The police still thought she had something to do with Lydia's murder. People in town believed that R. J. Rosen's books led someone to a copycat kill. And then there was R. J. Rosen himself…

Life imitates art.

Book four opened with Jordan still in bed while the police scoured Gap Lake for Crystal Lanier's killer.

Where Jordan herself was a sitting duck.

Addie's mind reeled. On page 17 Jordan was holed up in bed drinking tea and binge-watching *Dance Moms*. By page 41 she was in the clutches of a sadistic killer.

The story is just getting good.

Addie kicked off her blankets and pressed her bare feet into the carpet.

She wasn't going to be a sitting duck. She scrutinized her closet, passing by the cache of frilly things that Maya had talked her into, and instead going for what was easy, what was fast—what she could run in. She grabbed jeans and a T-shirt, tucking in the shirt so no one could grab her from behind. She slipped into sneakers and started gathering her hair into a ponytail, then paused. She remembered the instructor on some YouTube channel telling her that ponytails were like handles to pervs—easy to grab. She smoothed her hair, tucking it behind her ears. She threw a few air punches, bobbing and weaving like she'd seen on TV. On a whim she tossed in a roundhouse kick, got her sneaker stuck in the curtains, and brought the whole thing down, curtain, rod, and her entire body crashing to the floor.

She wasn't exactly a kick-ass heroine.

She took the stairs two at a time, bouncing gently on the foot that was stuck in the curtains.

"Well, you look chipper all of a sudden." Her father was sitting at the head of the table, leaning slightly back while Louisa heaped his plate with French toast. The smell—usually mouthwatering to Addie—turned her sour stomach.

"I'm feeling a little bit better."

Louisa pulled out a chair and started to fix Addie a plate. "No, thanks, Louisa. I'm just going to have an apple." Addie snatched one from the bowl on the counter and turned on her heel before either her father or Louisa could stop her.

She was on the front porch before she stopped talking, before her heart could register a normal pace.

"Hey, Addie."

She whirled, blinked, and Spencer grinned. "Sorry. It seems like I'm always freaking you out."

Addie shook her head, forced a smile. "I'm always a little freaky lately." Her cheeks burned a fierce red. "That came out wrong. Really, really wrong."

She expected Spencer to say something salacious or annoying; Colton would have.

"What are you doing here?"

"I was just…" He thumbed over his shoulder toward his car, parked in Colton's driveway.

"Oh, that's right. Your mom is Colton's mom's pusher."

Spencer's eyebrows shot up. "What was that?"

"Colton told me. Your mom sells leggings and stuff? He just called her…and your mom…" Addie could feel the heat creep over the tops of her ears. She knew she was blushing a fierce red, probably sweating satellites under her arms. "Sorry, this is really awkward. You have every right to be here."

She expected him to blow her off or take off running after her marathon blabbering. Instead he just shrugged. "You need a ride?"

TWENTY-EIGHT

Addie's head spun. Spencer Cohen was offering her a ride. Suddenly, her throat was dry and her heart was thundering in a different pattern. The angst-ridden terror was gone, overthrown by something sticky sweet.

Spencer Cohen wants to drive me to school.

Everything in Addie's brain screamed. He was a suspect in a murder. *But then again, so am I.* His ex-girlfriend was found dead less than a week ago! *Maybe he needs some company...*

Addie found herself nodding. She found herself shifting her backpack and pushing her hair back over her shoulder, the sexy, coy move she had seen Maya do a thousand times. She giggled. She batted her eyelashes. She hated herself.

Spencer grinned at her, a grin that was half joyful, half relieved. He darted around the car and pulled the passenger side door open for her. Addie wanted to sing. She wanted to dance and be gleeful and thrilled that a boy—not just any boy, *Spencer Cohen*—was fawning over her, but the darkness was still there, still playing at the back of her mind.

What if he was a murderer?

She sat down in his car, clicked on her seat belt, and sunk into the seat as he settled in his. Spencer tossed her another grin and turned over the ignition, his fingertips brushing over her shoulder as he backed out. Fireworks worked their way up Addie's spine.

This is okay, she told herself. I can feel this. I'm in a car with a boy. It's okay.

And both of us are being accused of murder.

Addie chewed on that last thought, doing her best to work it out of her mind.

They drove in silence for the first couple of miles, Addie gnawing her bottom lip and trying to look nonchalant and cool, Spencer tapping out the beat to every song on the radio on his steering wheel. The closer they got to Hawthorne High, the more the knot in Addie's chest tightened. Hawthorne was a big place, but news traveled fast. Would everyone know that the police had been to her door?

They had gone to Colton's too, she reminded herself. They said they were doing "due diligence" and following "leads." *But what lead had brought them to her door?* GapLakeLove.

R. J. Rosen.

Sucking in a breath she hoped Spencer didn't catch, Addie thumbed her phone open, glanced at the screen. She commended herself for keeping her cool when she saw the message.

TheRealRJRosen:

I'm watching you.

"Everything okay?" Spencer asked.

Addie nodded, certain that if she opened her mouth her heart would spill out. Finally, "Just my dad."

Spencer nodded. "He seems pretty cool. Is it just you and him?"

Again Addie nodded, mute.

"Must be kind of nice."

"I guess. He…he kind of works a lot."

Spencer nodded, turned the radio down a notch. "What does he do?"

"He's in finance. So, is your dad…better?"

Spencer's eyebrows went up. "You mean his drinking? Yeah, maybe if he admitted he had a problem he would be able to do something about it."

"Oh," Addie cleared her throat. "I'm sorry, I shouldn't have…"

Spencer shrugged and flashed her one of those three-point grins that felt like a lightning bolt. "No, no worries. Do I sound horrible talking about him? I'm sure I drive him crazy."

"Oh, I doubt that! You?" Addie cocked her head, pretty sure she was flirting, pretty sure she was nailing it. "You seem so…sweet."

Spencer's cheeks pinkened deliciously and Addie was suddenly a thousand miles away from her problems. She was in a car with a boy, with the windows rolled down, the music cranked up, and this boy was smiling—at her.

Spencer narrowed his eyes so that they crinkled at the corners. Somehow, the move only made his eyes sparkle more. His voice was a playful, throaty whisper. "I'm only sweet until you get to know me."

"I guess. I mean, I've seen you playing water polo!"

The color drained from Spencer's face and Addie's mouth went slack, her eyes bugging. "I didn't mean anything by that. I didn't mean…I mean, about the—I know it was an accident."

Quickly and coolly, Spencer went back to that easy smile, the sexy crinkle around his cocoa-brown eyes. "Oh, I wasn't worried about that. I was a little worried about you peeking at me in the swimming pool. Tell me, Addison Gaines, are you peeking at me anywhere else I should know about?"

Addie burned a fierce red. "I wasn't spying on you. I just saw you bringing stuff into Colton's house that one time. I wasn't staring. "

Spencer's laugh cut through the car. He slapped the steering wheel. "You're way too easy, Addie. I was just joking."

Addie's humiliation turned to annoyance. "Hey, maybe I'm on the neighborhood watch. Did you ever think of that? It's my duty to watch suspicious people moving stuff at night. You're lucky I didn't call the police. How do I know you weren't actually robbing Colton?"

Spencer eyed the road, was silent for a beat. "I suppose I should watch myself. I mean, what would the police say if they saw someone moving property *into* a house? That's practically robbery! Except it's the exact opposite of that because I'm putting stuff in, not taking stuff out."

Addie frowned. "You're making fun of me."

Spencer nodded. "Yes, I am."

"You suck."

"You're a peeping Tom."

"Maybe you should stay out of my neighborhood. What were you doing anyway?"

Spencer's eyes flicked from the street in front of them to Addie, then back again. Just the glance—a tiny, three-second glance—made her heart titter and ratcheted up her temperature by ten degrees.

"I'm just hanging out with Colton for a little bit. Dad is... being Dad."

"A safe house, nice."

Spencer was smiling as he pulled the car into the Hawthorne High parking lot. "It's possible you watch too many crime shows."

TWENTY-NINE

Maya was standing at the edge of the parking lot, gaping, when Addie approached her.

"Okay, you'd better start talking, like, right now, young lady."

Addie wrinkled her nose. "Young lady? I'm six months older than you."

"Don't try to change the subject. You're riding in cars with boys! You're riding in a car with a boy. Spencer Cohen."

Addie glanced nonchalantly over her shoulder even as everything inside her exploded. "Oh, yeah, I guess I was. Anyway, I should get to class." She took two tiny steps, pausing when Maya slapped a hand on her arm and yanked.

"No way. You'll tell me every last detail about your fictional boyfriend and your nonsexual love affair with an online author, but when it comes to a real, living, breathing boy you play coy? Not happening. Spill everything."

Addie's grin was so wide her ears hurt. "It's nothing, really. Spencer was just leaving Colton's house and he saw me and he offered me a ride."

"Just like that?"

"Just like that."

"And?"

Addie cocked out a hip. "And nothing. It was nice. We talked."

Maya was visibly crushed. "That's it? You talked? Was it at least super sexy pillow talk?"

Addie shook her head but didn't stop smiling. "No. It was just… nice." She shifted her backpack and started to walk toward her chemistry class.

"It was nice?" Maya spat. "Puppies are nice. Dinner with my grandma is nice. Being in a car with a hotsy-totsy like Spencer Cohen should be more than nice."

Addie raised an eyebrow. "A hotsy-totsy?"

Maya shrugged. "I did just have dinner with my grandma. Okay, now on to the real issue. Lydia Stevenson. You got a ride to school with Lydia Stevenson's ex-boyfriend. Did he say anything about her? Did he tell you he's secretly been harboring a burning love for you the whole time and that's why he had to send her to stepping?"

"'Send her to stepping'? Who are you?"

"I'm your best friend and because my life is currently devoid of love, and more importantly sex, I need to have all the details from my probably-going-to-do-it best friend."

Addie stopped. "How did I go from getting a ride to probably-going-to-do-it?"

Maya narrowed her eyes. "Just start talking."

Addie pulled open the door, and Maya edged in front of her, gesturing for Addie to start talking as they walked.

"He didn't say anything about Lydia. We didn't talk about her or relationships or anything. It was just a car ride to school, okay? Just that."

"Okay, but I bet it's the start of something romantic and totally hot."

Addie rolled her eyes but deep down hoped that Maya was right.

"All right everyone, take your seats. We have fifty-six minutes, not all day." Mr. Dawson was always in a hurry, convinced that his chemistry class would, at any minute, run out of time and self-destruct. "Take one and pass them back, please."

"You're seriously just going to leave me hanging?"

"I told you everything, Maya."

"Not the nuance. Not the...the...essence of the car ride."

"Girls, please!" Mr. Dawson pinned Addie with a glare, then droned on for fifteen minutes about the packet, about four days of homework, and about other things that Addie couldn't focus on. Spencer Cohen was single and he decided to drive *her* to school. That meant something, didn't it?

No, she scolded herself, *it didn't. He was outside and she was outside. They were going to the same place. Maybe he's just...what? An environmentalist? No, kind. He was just being nice to her.*

Addie wasn't sure why she was convincing herself.

"Something you'd care to share, Ms. Gaines?"

Addie blinked up at Mr. Dawson who was staring her down. She shook her head silently, certain that every single person in the classroom could hear what she was thinking. "No, sir," she said with a whisper.

* * *

Addie made it through the rest of her chemistry class unscathed and was for once happy that Maya wasn't in her government or art class. At least she'd have a two-hour reprieve from her best friend's needling, from Maya's constant barrage of questions and pronouncements of Spencer's intentions and the supposed near-death of Addie's virginity.

"He totally wants you," was the last thing that Maya had whispered in her ear after the chemistry bell rang. "He totally wants you and you want him and you guys are totally going to do it, and I'm going to die a virgin."

When the lunch bell rang, Addie's stomach was growling even though Hawthorne High was known for their all-gray lunch selections in the gruel line. Maya was waiting for her in front of the cafeteria doors.

"Are we having lunch, or do you and Spencer have plans?"

"You really need to get off this Spencer-and-me kick. It's getting way old."

Maya pushed out her lower lip. "Look, I've known you for two years and the only man-related thing that has ever happened to you is a new boy character in your Gap Lake fan fiction. This is big. This is my little girl growing up." She faked a sniffle.

"Spencer and I don't have plans, so you get to share my gray plate as usual."

Maya shot her a half smile. "Good. But seriously, why don't you whip out that credit card and door-dash us something delicious?"

"For emergencies only," Addie said.

Maya frowned. "My stomach is having an emergency."

"Maybe I should see what Spencer is doing…"

"So you do love him!"

Addie groaned. "Get a tray."

THIRTY

Addie followed Maya out into the hall later that day, Maya rooting through her backpack. "I totally killed that quiz," Maya said.

"So you won't have to live off me after all," Addie said. She paused, putting her hand on Maya's shoulder. "Also, can you not say kill? I just"—she shuddered—"I'm still freaked out."

"Sorry, Adds. I guess I am too."

"This whole thing is just…I mean, I can't believe something like that happened here."

Maya shrugged. "This school is not exactly known for its lively student body. It's been a long time, but…"

Addie shook her head. She knew the legends. Hawthorne High bred some kind of madness.

"I thought that was all in the past."

"Yeah, well, let's not get ahead of ourselves. Um, hello, stare much?" Maya glared at the group of girls who had stopped in the hallway and were eying Addie and Maya. They turned away and Addie shifted her backpack.

"That was weird. I feel like everyone is staring at me."

They were.

"I mean, I saw her get out of his car this morning. I mean, who does that?" One of the girls whispered loudly.

Addie felt heat at the back of her neck.

"Are they talking about me?"

Maya roped her arm through Addie's and tried to pull her along. Addie stayed rooted, her stomach clenched, her saliva going sour.

"Spencer and Lydia broke up months ago," the other girl said, brushing her fingers through her curly brown hair.

"But he decides to move on, like, *days* after his ex-girlfriend died? That's just morbid."

"Maybe he didn't decide to move on. Maybe Addie decided to move *in*."

Addie shook Maya off. "They're talking about me and Spencer."

"So there is an Addie and Spencer," the first girl said with a sharp grin. "I knew it."

Maya stepped up. "What are you miscreants talking about?"

"We aren't the only ones talking about it. Lydia Stevenson turns up dead, then, like, days later, Addie Gaines, the chick who spends all of her free time writing about morbid death and murder, moves in on her boyfriend. That's sick."

Heat exploded at the back of Addie's eyes. She shook her head, trying to force herself to talk, to make some sort of sense.

"No," was all she could muster. "No, no, it's not like that."

"So it's not like you write about murder and then one happens— kind of like the ones all over your website?"

Addie's stomach folded in on itself.

"Do people really think that?"

"People really think that you may have had something to do with Lydia's murder, yeah."

"Shut up! That's not true and you know it." Maya exploded, her cheeks a dark red.

The girls shrugged and skulked off down the hall, slowing every once in a while to shoot withering glances back at Addie and Maya.

"Maya, I can't believe—"

"No one believes that you killed Lydia, Adds."

"They do!"

"Who are they? No one! Anyone who believes that you could actually kill someone because you write about it is stupid. That's not how murder works. That's not—that's just not real."

Addie tried to swallow, tried to force her breath back to normal. "The lady on the news said there might be a copycat killer."

"Listen to me." Maya stopped dead in the center of the hall, turning Addie to face her. The weight of her hands felt good on Addie's shoulders, felt solid and real. "That woman was just a nosy concerned citizen. She's not a police officer or any kind of psychologist or anything like that. She's just espousing stupid beliefs. No one—except for those two idiots in the hall—thinks that you have anything to do with what happened to Lydia."

Addie tried to nod. She tried to force a smile, but her lips were bone dry and she could feel the skin stretch and break. "I didn't do it."

"I know that, Addie. Everyone knows that."

"But...she may have been killed because of me."

Addie could tell that Maya was trying to restrain herself. She could feel her best friend's fingertips burrowing into her skin. "What are you talking about?"

"R. J.—"

"Don't even start with that, Addie."

A dark thought began to form at the edge of her periphery.

I'm watching you...

Addie spun, her breath catching in her throat.

"He could be here."

"What? Who?"

"R. J. Rosen."

"Addie..."

Addie shrugged Maya's hands off her and held up her own. "Hear me out," she started. "We don't know who R. J. Rosen is. No one really does. I always just assumed he was some big-shot writer in New York."

"But?"

"But what if he's not?"

Maya shook her head. "I don't understand. What are you talking about?"

Addie slipped her phone out of her back pocket. "You said it yourself. What if it's Mr. Moreau?"

Maya forced an uncomfortable laugh. "And you said that was stupid. And you were right."

"But look." She opened the Google search engine and typed in R. J. Rosen's name.

"So there are, like, fifty million results. I'd say that makes him pretty available."

"No." Addie thumbed through the list, clicking on one after the other. "It's all basically the same information, and it's all—"

"Pretty useless."

"Exactly. Why I write, what I write about, how I research."

Maya pulled out her phone. "He has to have an 'about the author' page or whatever, right?" She went to his site and frowned. "There's one from his publisher and one from Amazon, and neither have a picture."

Addie scrolled through her phone. "Here's a Wikipedia page."

"No picture." Maya crossed her arms. "I'm still not sure what any of this means."

Addie slid her phone back into her pocket and stepped closer to Maya, lowering her voice. "It means that R. J. Rosen could be anyone. He could be a teacher here, or maybe even a student."

"He could be a she."

Addie's eyes flashed and her jaw clenched.

"I didn't mean you!"

"I know…"

"But I'm still not sure what you're getting at. Even if R. J. Rosen were a teacher here or something, what does it have to do with Lydia?"

Addie shook her head. "What if…what if it isn't a copycat? What if the person who killed Lydia and the person who is writing to me are the same person?"

"R. J. Rosen?"

"Someone who wants me to think he's R. J. Rosen."

THIRTY-ONE

The girls walked to the cafeteria in stony silence. Addie's head was spinning; she was trying to think of the emails, the story posts from R. J. Could it be possible that he was stalking her? Could he have killed Lydia? But why?

None of it made sense.

"I think we should leave," Maya said, stopping in the cafeteria doorway. "Let's go eat out front. You weren't in the mood for anything cafeteria-gray anyway, were you?" She dug in her backpack. "I have gummy worms and Tic Tacs. Taste the rainbow."

"Neither of those sound a whole heck of a lot better than a gray cheeseburger." Addie tried to reach around her. "Come on."

"Don't go in there."

"What? Why?"

"Just—"

Addie stepped into the cafeteria, and it was like stepping into a silent movie where she was the star—or the villain. Conversations broke. Utensils stopped in midair. Heads swung to face her. Eyes narrowed.

Addie swallowed.

"What's…?"

"Let's just go." Maya threaded her arm through Addie's and gave her a yank.

"Everyone was just staring at me. Everyone. Maya, they hate me."

"No." Maya shook her head. "No."

Was it possible that the whole school could turn against her that quickly?

"I just got in the car with Spencer…"

Maya sucked in a breath. "It's the blog too."

Addie's face went ashen. "My blog?"

"People saw the pictures, Addie. And I know you didn't have anything to do with them, I do. I know you would never do something like that. But the pictures, and the last few stories, and now Spencer. People are just talking. But that's all it is, stupid talk. It'll blow over tomorrow, I know."

Addie bit back tears. "Will it? Lydia is dead."

"And you had nothing to do with that. My parents are going to find the real sicko who did this and lock him up, and everyone's going to go on with their lives. I promise."

"People really think…"

"Forget about it, Addie."

She swallowed hard, saliva that tasted like hot metal. "Why didn't you tell me everyone hated me?"

"They don't. I don't. It'll blow over. Everyone will realize how ridiculous they're being and things will be back to normal before you know it."

Addie stepped back from Maya, shaking her head. "No, no it won't. Nothing is ever going to be the same again."

Addie left Maya behind in the hall, tears shaking her shoulders. She dialed her father once, twice, three times. He never answered, she never bothered to leave a message. When the bell rang, Addie did her best to melt into the ugly off-white paint in the hallway, but eyes continued to peer. No one pointed fingers—no one had to. The accusation was in their stares, in the way their eyes cut over her, through her. It was in the way that people she had spent years in school with suddenly gave her a wide berth, suddenly shifted away when she came through.

After she spent fifth period in the bathroom, she called Louisa, begged her to pick her up. Before she did, Addie messaged Maya.

AddieGaines:

I'm going home. Can't stand this.

MayaPumpkinPYA:

U didn't do anything wrong!

AddieGaines:

Doesn't matter. Everyone hates me.

MayaPumpkinPYA:

No1 does.

Addie paused, sucked in a breath and glanced at the clock.

It would take Louisa close to thirty minutes to reach her. Each minute felt like an hour.

AddieGaines:

> R. J. wants me to post something else.

MayaPumpkinPYA:

> But UR not going 2, right?

AddieGaines:

> He said I'd be sorry.

MayaPumpkinPYA:

> Fuck him. You'll be sorry if you do.

AddieGaines:

> I know, I won't. Call me later?

"I'll do you one better."

Maya was standing in the junior hall ladies' room, grinning at Addie.

"How did you know where I was?"

Maya dangled her phone. "Find My Friends app."

"That's creepy."

She shrugged. "I'll take it off when I have a boyfriend to inappropriately stalk. You okay? Need a hug?"

"I will be and yes."

Maya grabbed Addie in a giant bear hug. "Can't. Breathe," she gasped. Maya released her and Addie stepped back, admiring her friend. "That coat looks way better on you than it did on me."

Maya beamed. "I wasn't going to say anything, but I think so too." She pulled the hood up, the faux fur lining nearly engulfing her entire face.

"I can't even see you in there."

"I know, *très* mysterious, right?" She reached for Addie's hand. "Come on."

"Where are you going?"

"I'm driving you home. My car's fixed."

"We've got two more classes and I have a note." Addie held up the hastily scribbled note she had obtained from the school nurse when she feigned cramps. "If you cut, your parents will put you in a holding cell."

Maya narrowed her eyes. "That was just rude. Well, at the very least, I'm walking out in solidarity with you."

"You can't!"

Maya held up a toilet seat painted in hot pink, bold black letters reading MR. H's BATHROOM PASS stenciled across the seat. "I have a pass too. For a few minutes at least. Come on."

Addie and Maya walked out of Hawthorne High.

"You know, for every cop in the county tromping through here, security is pretty lax."

Maya blinked. "My parents have better things to do. They're trying to catch a killer."

Addie sucked in a breath. "I just can't believe…"

Maya squeezed Addie's elbow.

"It's freezing out here." Addie struggled to pull up the hood on the new-old jacket she got from Maya's car.

"You're stuck on your backpack," Maya said, pulling the pack off Addie's shoulder and slinging it over her own. "You sure you're going to be okay?"

"No, but at least if I'm at home I know…" What? That she was safe? "I don't know. Hey, there's Louisa."

Maya followed Addie across the street, waiting until Addie slid into Louisa's car.

"Love you, okay?"

Maya blew her an air kiss. "Take care."

Louisa turned the key in the ignition, the engine giving a slight purr. She jutted her chin toward Maya and waved, then told Addie, "I almost couldn't tell you two apart. Isn't that your coat?"

Addie nodded. "Maya's borrowing it. Can we just go home? I don't feel so well."

Louisa gave a curt nod and flicked her blinker on as Maya waved back and stepped into the crosswalk in front of Louisa's car. The heat was blowing and Addie was already starting to sweat; she was wrestling with her jacket so she didn't see the car on the other side of the street.

She didn't hear its engine roar.

She didn't see it veer from the curb.

She didn't see it gain speed.

But she saw it hit her best friend.

THIRTY-TWO

Everything fell into sickening slow motion. The car, the way its headlight clipped Maya. The sound of flesh hitting metal. Addie watched in horror as her friend was swept off her feet, one sneaker never making it off the ground.

Maya went up, clawing at the air. Her hood flew off and Addie could see her face, could see the screwed-up, terrified twist of her lips as she opened her mouth. She looked like she was screaming, but there was only silence.

Then Maya hit the car.

Her hip, first.

She spun, palms outstretched, *eek*ing across the top of the car. And then she was gone.

"Maya!" Addie screamed, clawing at the door, throwing her full body weight against it. She was desperate to get out, to get to Maya. Tears were running down her cheeks, snot and sweat running over her lips.

"Maya, no!"

She kicked the door open and that action seemed to vault

the world into hyper speed. Sounds were suddenly deafening: the screech of the tires as the car cleared Maya and disappeared around a corner. The thundering of Addie's own heart as it slammed against her rib cage. The ragged claw of her breath. She was running, her sneakers making flat slapping sounds against the pavement.

"Maya, Maya, Maya…" she murmured.

She wasn't in the road.

Addie scanned, her breath catching in her throat, her stomach going to liquid. Maya had been tossed clear across the street and was laying in the gutter, one shoe off, her body curled and bent like a question mark. Her backpack was gone, books scattered across the street, fluttering like grotesque butterflies in the snapping wind. Addie launched herself toward Maya.

"Maya, Maya!"

She crumpled to the ground but stopped short of touching her. Maya's body was radiating a deep heat. Her eyes were half closed but her lips were moving, though no sound came out.

"Maya, please, no, you have to stay with me."

Maya was sucking in air now, her chest rising and falling with a rapid speed that Addie wasn't used to. Was that normal? Did Maya always breathe so fast? Was that good?

She gingerly reached out to cradle Maya's cheek, and Maya's head lolled toward her, feeling heavy in her hand.

"Don't touch her!" Louisa was saying, moving across the street. "Don't move her at all, you might hurt her worse."

But Addie had Maya's head in both her hands, a trickle of blood from Maya's nose rolling over her cheek and staining Addie's fingers a brilliant, terrifying red.

She had her best friend's blood on her hands. Literally.

"This is my fault," Addie whispered, moving the fur-lined hood so it cradled Maya's head better. "I'm so, so sorry."

Maya was still breathing, but her eyelids were fluttering like she was struggling to stay awake, stay alive.

"Please, no," Addie was saying, her whole body racked with a tremor that made her teeth chatter. "Please don't die."

Maya's lips puckered and sputtered. "I'm not going to die," she said, her voice a raspy, choked whisper. "I'm not going to die, right?"

Addie blinked away tears and shook her head. "No, no, you're not going to die." She could already see the bloom of bruises forming on Maya's cheeks, around her eyes. She didn't dare look any further, didn't want to see a telltale pool of blood or a leg splayed at a weird angle.

"You're going to be fine," Addie said, her teeth gritted so hard her jaw ached. "You're not going to die. This wasn't meant for you, Maya. It wasn't."

"What are you talking—"

"Shh." Addie used the back of her hand to wipe away her tears, sniffed hard. "Don't talk, just relax."

The tiniest hint of a smile played on Maya's lips. "I'm in the gutter. You relax."

Addie couldn't help the guffaw that came out of her mouth. Maya was going to be okay.

"I've called 911," Louisa was saying, holding up her phone as if Addie needed proof. "They're on their way. Are you okay, Maya?"

Maya closed her eyes, wincing. "Everything hurts."

Addie gingerly fingered the fabric covering Maya's arm. It was streaked with mud from the street, caked with dirt. The white faux fur around Maya's wrists was half gray, a thread of red running through it. Addie absently went to brush it away. She sucked on her teeth when she realized it was blood.

"Oh God, you're bleeding."

"Probably," Maya moaned.

Addie didn't want to look at her best friend, but she had to meet her eyes. Maya's lids fluttered open for a half second and Addie could see that her eyes were red-rimmed, glassy. When she closed her eyes again, a single tear fall.

"Why did this happen?" she said in that low, choked whisper.

"I don't think it was supposed to happen to you," Addie said, the words burning her tongue. "I think it was supposed to happen to me."

* * *

It seemed to take hours for the police and ambulance to show up, and Addie remained crouched by Maya's side, her hand on Maya's cheek, her other one stroking her arm, gently patting her hand.

"You're going to be fine, you're going to be fine," she kept repeating.

Louisa paced behind her, wringing her hands and occasionally giving Addie soft pats on the shoulder, on her back.

The ring of the Hawthorne bell was almost drowned out by the drone of the police sirens, the wail of the ambulance. Addie looked up, stunned as students filed out of the building, began populating the front lawn in front of the school, stopping, staring. *Pointing.* They were pointing.

THIRTY-THREE

Terror and humiliation thrummed through her. They were pointing. They were whispering.

They probably thought I did this.

The tears fell in a torrent, Addie's shoulders rocking with each sob.

You did *do this.*

R. J. Rosen said she needed to post "or else."

Addie looked over Maya, her form crumpled, the rapid rise and fall of her chest a slow plod. *Was this "or else"?*

Her whole body went cold, the world fish-eyeing as her knees buckled. She saw the flash, heard the squeal of the ambulance slamming to a stop. She heard car doors slamming, people yelling, feet slamming against concrete. Addie's knees buckled. Her shoulder hit the concrete first, sending white-hot flashes of pain up her arms, across her back, but it felt good to ache, felt good to hurt. Her friend was lying in a heap and she was responsible. Addie's hands slammed against the street next, pebbles and the broken asphalt slicing through the flesh on her palms. She winced but relished the fiery heat of skin tearing, the sticky feeling of blood seeping across her skin. She needed it.

"Addie! Are you okay?"

She felt Louisa gather her up, shaking her gently and patting her cheeks.

"Do you need assistance here?" Addie blinked up at a navy-blue-clad paramedic, his plastic kit swinging by his side.

"Maya," she whispered. "You need to get to Maya." She blinked in the streak of sunlight, pointed toward Maya.

"She's already being attended to."

Addie squinted and saw that a team of paramedics were carefully but quickly putting a neck brace on Maya, then sliding her onto a board. Addie tried to swallow the lump in her throat, but the tears were already at her eyes. "Is she going to be okay?"

The paramedic nodded. "We don't know much, but she's alert and talking. That's always a good sign."

"Addie!"

Addie sat up, let Louisa pull her to her feet. Detective Garcia and Chief Garcia arrived in separate cars, the detective stepping back as the paramedics moved Maya into the back of the ambulance.

"What happened?"

Addie started to heave. She cried big, rollicking cries until they strangled her, until her throat ached.

Detective Garcia leaned down to her, his big hands on her arms. His eyes were wide, laser focused, but there was a kindness in them. "Slow down. Can you tell me anything?"

"A car. I was leaving school because I didn't feel well and Maya was just walking with me. She…Louisa was here waiting to pick me up and I got in her car. Then Maya crossed the street and…"

The accident replayed again in her head.

But it wasn't an accident.

Someone meant to hit Maya. Someone knew exactly what they were going to do.

No.

They didn't mean to hit Maya.

They meant to hit *her*.

"The car came out of nowhere and hit her. They didn't even stop—they didn't even slow down."

The tears were soaking the collar of her shirt, leaving an itchy trail on her neck.

"What did the car look like? Do you remember?"

Addie shook her head miserably, squeezing her eyes shut and clenching her jaw. She should know this. She saw it, she saw every inch of ground the car covered. She heard the sickening thud…

"Blue, maybe? Or black? I—I don't remember. It happened so fast. Maybe Louisa remembers?"

Louisa swallowed slowly and leaned into the Detective, muttering a few words that sounded like gibberish to Addie.

"Are you okay, Addison?"

It was Maya's mother then, jogging over. She was wearing her uniform, the walkie-talkie clamped to her shoulder barking with commands and numbers that Addie didn't understand.

"She doesn't know what the car looked like," Detective Garcia told his wife. His voice was even, but Addie could feel the frustration rolling off him.

"That's okay. That's okay, it's a lot to think about right now. First of all, let's get you out of the street."

Addie let the Garcias lead her to the curb, then sank down. "You shouldn't be here with me. You should be with Maya. Is she…is she…" Addie couldn't say it. She wouldn't. The paramedic had said that Maya was alert, was talking, that that was a "good sign." But Addie didn't believe anything anymore.

"She's going to be fine," Chief Garcia assured her. "If you can remember, where was the car coming from?"

Addie pointed. "It was parked right there. I remember that. It was parked."

"Okay, good. Can you remember the make of the car?"

She shook her head, a tear rolling down her cheek. "I don't know. I don't know cars. I don't even drive. All I know is he was at the curb, I think. I'm sure. No, I'm pretty sure. He was at the curb in front of the school and then he was…he was…the car just hit Maya."

"You said 'he.' Did you see the driver?"

Addie shook her head miserably. "No."

"Chief Garcia? Detective? We're ready to take Maya to the hospital now."

The detective glanced back at Addie, then gave the paramedic a sharp nod. "I'll ride with her."

"I'm right behind her," the Chief said.

Addie watched Maya's parents in a brief embrace before they got into their separate vehicles and took Maya to the hospital, leaving Addie and Louisa standing on the curb.

"I want to go to the hospital."

Louisa shook her head. "They won't let you see her anyway, at least not yet. Best that you come home, especially if you're feeling sick. It'll be okay."

Addie didn't move when Louisa tugged her by the arm. She stayed rooted, watching the police cars, listening to the engines turn over one by one as they backed out and pulled away. Once they were gone, it was like nothing ever happened except for Maya's shoe, left there in the road. Addie darted across the street to grab it. As she stood up, she saw that there were still a handful of students lingering, staring.

You'll post or else. R. J. Rosen was still haunting her.

THIRTY-FOUR

Louisa pulled into the driveway and let Addie out of the car.

"Wait, I'll come in."

Addie shook her head. It had been throbbing since she'd gotten back in Louisa's car. He throat ached from constant crying, and her eyes felt like she had rubbed them with sandpaper. "I'm okay."

Louisa set her jaw and looked Addie over. "You shouldn't be alone."

Addie just shrugged and slammed the car door, trudging up the front porch. She had to think. Louisa sat in the front seat of her car and stared out; she waited a beat then picked up her phone. Addie was sure the woman was texting her father.

She shut the door behind her with a soft click, loving the cool emptiness of the house. It was cavernous and dark; just the way Addie felt. Her hands were shaking, a violent tremor that went up her arms and sunk deep into her bones. She could hear her teeth chatter as she sunk to the floor, hugging her knees to her chest.

Maya was lying in a hospital bed somewhere, probably hooked up to a thousand wires. It should have been Addie. She tried to cry, but there was nothing there. Instead, she pulled out her cell phone and dialed her best friend.

Addie's heart thudded with each ring. She was going to hang up when she heard, "Addie?"

Her breath caught, like a fist to her gut. "Chief Garcia. Is...is Maya all right?"

The police chief sucked in a deep sigh and Addie felt the tension pulsing through her. "She is, yes. We're actually taking her home right now."

Elation, like a hot spark, shot through Addie. "Can I talk to her?"

"Honey, I don't think that would be the best."

"Please? Please? I just need to know that she's all right."

I just need to know that she doesn't blame me.

Addie heard murmuring on Chief Garcia's end of the phone. There was a muffled fumbling, then Maya's voice, still soft, still raspy. "Addie?"

"Oh thank God, Maya, I thought you were—"

"Dead? Me too."

Addie smiled even as fresh tears made tracks down her cheeks. "I'm so sorry."

"For what? You weren't driving."

Addie pressed her finger into the soft flesh of her arm, watching the way the blood drained, leaving an oblong white O on her flesh. "I think that car was meant for me."

"How do you know that?"

Addie worried her bottom lip, pinched the bridge of her nose where the thud of her headache thumped like a snare drum. "Think about it: you were wearing my coat."

"And?"

"And everyone in school thinks I'm a murderer."

"So you think they were trying to wipe you out? Addie, that doesn't make sense even in your twisted, Gap Lake–stained mind."

Addie's stomach felt leaden at the mention of Gap Lake. "And R. J. Rosen…" She could practically hear Maya roll her eyes.

"And R. J. Rosen nothing. He sent you some emails, Adds. He's not your guardian angel."

"I don't think he's a guardian at all, Maya. I think he's evil."

"And completely out of his mind?"

"What are you talking about?"

Maya snort laughed, then seemed to wince. "Ow. Remind me not to laugh, even at you. Addie, I was wearing your coat. Totally true. I'm also darker than you are, have way better hair, and basically go up to your waist. If someone was gunning for you and thought that I was you, then you're in the clear. Your stalker is a damn idiot."

"Maya, I—"

She wanted to tell Maya that the emails had turned sinister.

"Addie," Chief Garcia cut her off. "Maya really needs to rest. We're headed home."

"Oh, then I'll come over and meet you there. Is that okay?"

There was a slight, soft pause. "I don't think so."

"But—"

The phone clicked in her ear, the silence deafening.

Addie took the stairs two at a time. She fired up her laptop, pulled up all the emails from R. J. Rosen, and hit Print. She paused when the printer spat out the last page, then turned back to her screen.

AddieGaines:

I'm not posting anything else.

TheRealRJRosen:

You promised.

AddieGaines:

I told you I was done and I am. I'm deleting the GapLakeLove site too. Don't contact me ever again.

TheRealRJRosen:

That sounds very, very serious.

AddieGaines:

Just stop. I'm going to the police.

TheRealRJRosen:

With what?

AddieGaines:

Everything. All your emails, your posts, everything.

TheRealRJRosen:

I write fiction. All the stories I sent you were complete works of fiction.

AddieGaines:

Aren't you the one who said, "Life Imitates Art"?

TheRealRJRosen:

Clever girl! What I should have said was "Art Imitates Death." How's your little friend by the way?

Addie's blood went cold. She whirled around, suddenly feeling eyes on her, eyes everywhere. She yanked down the blinds, pulled the curtains.

AddieGaines:

How do you know about Maya?

TheRealRJRosen:

I'm the omniscient narrator. I know all. I control all.

AddieGaines:

Stupid. I'm going to the police and they're going to lock your ass up in jail.

TheRealRJRosen:

Or yours.

AddieGaines:

Meaning?

TheRealRJRosen:

Who's the real writer here?

AddieGaines:

Fuck you.

TheRealRJRosen:

You know in the book when the pretty young ingénue goes to the police? What happens?

Addie started to type, tried to log out, but another message came through.

TheRealRJRosen:

She only makes things worse. It's only going to get worse for you, Addie.

THIRTY-FIVE

Addie slammed her laptop shut, the bile itching at the back of her throat. She unplugged the thing and dumped it in her backpack, yanking handfuls of R. J.'s emails and messages from the printer tray and shoving those in too. She tried to steal herself, to catch her breath, but her heart was hammering like a fire bell, heat bursting behind her eyes, the ache of her head like a scythe scraping along her brain.

"Fuck you, R. J. Rosen," she muttered to herself. "Fuck you, whoever you are."

Addie bounded down the stairs and out the front door, stopping on the porch. Louisa wasn't there. Her father wasn't there. She spun, helpless, then pulled out her phone, finger hovering over the Zap Car app. She had used Zap a dozen times before; they were the only car service that came out to Black Rock Hills Estates, but something about calling a stranger and slipping into his car felt wrong. She had no idea who R. J. Rosen was.

He had told her it was going to get worse.

What if he drove the Zap Car?

She spotted Colton's car snaking up the main road. He slowed in front of her house, gave her a finger wave before pulling into his driveway.

Once he got out, he made a beeline for Addie. "Is Maya okay?"

Addie nodded, pulling her hair back into a ponytail. "She's going to be okay. Did you see what happened?"

He shook his head. "Not really. Did someone actually hit her?"

She nodded. "Yeah. I didn't see it all—didn't see everything. I mean...I should have."

"Hey." Colton reached out, laid one of his big hands on Addie's shoulder, and squeezed gently. "Don't be like that."

"Like what?"

"You're beating yourself up. This wasn't your fault."

If you only knew...

"I just feel responsible. Maya wouldn't have even been out there if it wasn't for me. She was walking me out because...because I just couldn't deal."

Colton's ice-blue eyes were sharp and he pinned Addie with a gaze. "First of all, the only person responsible for hurting Maya was the idiot in the Dodge. That's it. You didn't hit her, you didn't cause it."

Addie could feel the prick behind her eyes again. "You don't understand, Colton." She sniffed, using the back of her hand to swipe at her nose. "Maya was wearing my jacket. She looked just like me. I mean, a little shorter, but her hood was up and I think...I really think the person who hit her was aiming for me. He thought he was going to hit me."

Colton narrowed his eyes. "Why would you think that? Why would anyone hit either of you unless he was drunk or high or something?"

Addie dropped her head, studied the toes of her shoes. "People think I killed Lydia, Colton."

He reached out, clamped a hand on her wrist so quickly it startled Addie. "No one thinks that."

"Everyone thinks that. Why do you think I left school? Everyone was staring and people were talking. They think that because I was with Spencer this morning and because of the site and the fan fiction…"

"That's stupid. Addie. I've known you almost my whole life and I know you would never do anything like that. You couldn't hurt a fly."

Addie chuckled despite her tears. "You've known me for three years."

"That's what I said, like, my whole life." He cocked his head, eyes soft, half smile pushing up one apple cheek. "Trust me: no one actually believes that you had anything to do with Lydia's death. And no one was trying to mow you down to get some kind of literary revenge."

Addie knew Colton was joking, but the stupid phrase "literary revenge" sent a cold shiver down her spine. She considered telling Colton about R. J. Rosen, about the creepy messages. About the one that said it was "only going to get worse for her." She shook herself. "I really don't know what to believe anymore, but I need help."

"Okay." Colton spread his legs, put his fists on his hips, Superman style. "I'm your man. What do you need?"

"A ride?"

He gestured toward his car. "I can totally do that. Your chariot awaits, miss."

Addie smiled and followed Colton to his funky car, wrinkling her nose when she got in. She stared out the passenger side window, then rolled it down quickly. She knew teen boys smelled. She knew that Colton wasn't exactly known for his excellent hygiene practices. He wasn't an athlete, but his car smelled like an unholy combination of gym socks and blue cheese. Even with the fresh air whistling in the through the window, the stench was powerful.

"Look, I am so thankful that you're helping me right now, but I have to tell you Colton, your car stinks."

A flit of red shot across Colton's cheeks, but he smiled anyway. "You sound like everyone I know when you say that." He shrugged. "And really, it's an easy fix. I just have to find the sandwich or sneakers or rat that's rotting somewhere in here."

Addie scooted to the edge of the seat. "There's a dead rat in here?"

"It's most likely a dead cheeseburger, but I like to cover all my bases. Where did you say we were going?"

"To the police station."

Colton paled at the mention of the police.

"You okay?" Addie asked, touching his arm.

He forced a laugh that was tinny and unnatural, shaking Addie's hand off and batting at the air. "Yeah, totally. It's just—it was a long time ago. Me and the po-po are like"—he knitted his fingers together—"cool now."

Addie bit back a smile, trying her best to stifle it.

Colton narrowed his eyes. "What?"

"Nothing."

"I was fourteen."

Addie pursed her lips together.

"It was a stupid prank. A bunch of seniors dared me to. I didn't know the conviction would"—Addie could see the quirk of a smile at the edges of Colton's lips now too—"stick."

Addie snorted, a wild loud guffaw. "Then you shouldn't have used superglue!" She sputtered laughing, tears rollicking over her cheeks.

"They said, 'Moon the cops.' How was I supposed to know they'd superglue my cheeks to the windshield? It's not that funny, you know." But Colton was smiling. "That shit hurt."

"I heard it took four officers to free your ass."

Colton clucked his tongue. "Lies. It was six officers and two firefighters. Like you've never done anything crazy."

Addie shook her head, wiped the tears from her eyes. "Clean slate here. I'm just a nice girl."

"Yeah?" Colton asked, head cocked.

Addie bit her bottom lip. "Yeah."

She jumped when her phone pinged, the humor dropping immediately. Colton jutted his chin toward the phone in Addie's hand. "Do you need to get that?"

Addie gritted her teeth, her saliva tasting bitter. She didn't want to look. She didn't want to see R. J. Rosen's response.

The phone pinged again.

"Someone's insistent," Colton said with a slight grin.

Addie chanced a glance down at the screen of her phone, heartbeat thudding to a stop when she saw the name.

Spencer Cohen.

Spencer.

Addie couldn't stop the smile that shot across her lips. She couldn't stop the wash of guilt either, hearing the whispers of those girls from school: she's moving in on a dead girl's ex.

She slid open her phone, blinked at the message.

Spencer:

> Saw you outside school. Just wanted to make sure you were ok.

AddieGaines:

> Yeah, thank you. Maya got hit but she's going to be fine.

They drove in silence for a beat, Colton tapping his long fingers on the steering wheel. "So… Why are we going to the police station?"

Addie looked away, studying the view out the window, inching her finger along the hard plastic there. "I—I think I have some information about Lydia's murder." She swung her head to face Colton, to gauge his reaction. His face remained unchanged.

"Really?"

"I've been getting some really weird texts and emails and…"

"You think they're from Lydia's killer?"

Addie shrugged. "Maybe."

Colton dropped into silence for a beat, then cleared his throat. "You know the police have cleared Spencer."

Addie blinked. "I didn't know that, but I figured they would. I mean, he's...he's cool and really nice." She shot him a small smile, but Colton wouldn't look at her, his eyes glued to the huge, empty expanse in front of them. "I guess." Then, "Hey, I've got to be somewhere in a half hour..."

"Oh, sure, of course. I can totally get a ride home from the police department. I don't even—I mean, they might not even listen to anything I have to say. It does sound kind of crazy."

"So, who's this person who's been emailing you?"

Addie swallowed hard. "He says he's R. J. Rosen."

Colton flipped on his blinker, cruised smoothly into the police station parking lot.

"You don't think it's really him?"

Addie shook her head, embarrassment washing over her. "No."

"Why would someone pretend to be an author?"

"To punish me."

Colton pursed his lips, looking Addie over. He looked like he wanted to comment but shrugged instead.

Addie put her hand on his shoulder. "It sounds stupid, doesn't it?"

Colton didn't say anything. "If it helps find Lydia's killer, it can't be stupid, right?" He flashed a small smile.

She let herself out of the car. "Thanks, Colton."

"Good luck, Addie."

THIRTY-SIX

Addie stepped into the police department vestibule feeling immediately uncomfortable and—guilty? *I have nothing to feel guilty about,* she scolded herself.

Except that you're the reason Lydia is dead. You're the reason Maya is lying in a hospital bed somewhere.

No.

Maya was at home. Addie had heard her voice and she was fine.

If you could consider someone nearly made a hood ornament by a Dodge fine…

Addie paused, something needling at the back of her neck.

How did she know it was a Dodge that hit Maya?

She didn't.

But Colton did.

Addie turned, palms pressing against the glass, craning her head and staring out for Colton. She yanked the doors open, nearly taking out an officer on the walkway.

"Hey, relax, kid!"

"I'm so sorry—I was looking for my friend. Did you see him? He was driving a red car."

"What kind of car?"

Addie blinked. She didn't know. She didn't know what kind of car had been parked in front of Colton's house for the last year and a half. She shrugged, feeling immediately stupid. "A red one."

The officer looked over his shoulder, gaze sweeping the empty lot. "I don't see a red car out here."

"Thanks," Addie said in a low voice choked with embarrassment.

What did it mean that Colton knew what kind of car hit Maya? The bell had rung after Maya went down; the car was long gone by the time the students filed out onto the lawn. Addie's stomach dropped.

The smell in Colton's car.

Swampy.

She knew that smell.

It was coming from the journalism room.

It was coming from Lydia Stevenson's body.

Addie turned around, stared through the glass of the police station doors. She watched the officers inside hustling around, her stomach churning. What should she do? She couldn't walk into the police station and accuse her next-door neighbor of murder.

Colton's car smelled. Lots of people had smelly cars, but that didn't make them murderers. But he knew—or possibly knew—the make of the car that hit Maya even though he said he hadn't seen the accident. And where would he have gotten a Dodge anyway? Addie may not have known the make of Colton's car, but it was red. And his mother drove a fancy minivan that was always kept shiny black. His father? Addie didn't know except that it was a white car.

I'm being stupid.

This isn't about me, she reminded herself. *It's about Lydia.*

Lydia, crumpled on her desk, long hair hanging over her arm, skimming the dirty linoleum. Each time the image flashed, it seemed to burn deeper into her, boring a spot in her soul and making her stomach sour.

I had nothing to do with Lydia's death.

Unless it really was a copycat.

"Can I help you?"

Addie blinked at the police officer who appeared in the vestibule before her. She was hanging on the door, rocking forward on one foot. Then, she smiled. "Addie Gaines, right?"

Addie pumped her head. "I'm...I'm here about what happened. At the school that night."

Officer Chadwick stepped aside and ushered Addie through the door. "Come on in."

Addie glanced around the department. In the Gap Lake books, the police department was state of the art even though Gap Lake was basically a resort town. There were always officers working and a bank of computers and the occasional petty thief handcuffed in one of the waiting rooms. But the Crescent City police department was different. It was part doctor's waiting room, part principal's office. Coke machines blinking in one corner. Coffee machine with a stack of Styrofoam cups in the other. Bank of fluorescent lights buzzing

HANNAH JAYNE

overhead, and four desks that looked like they might have been new right about the time Addie was born. Officer Chadwick went to the nearest desk, pulled out a chair for Addie, and sat across from her.

"What can I do for you?"

Addie pulled her purse into her lap, feeling the edges of the latest Gap Lake book through the soft leather. "Well, I think I might have some information about Lydia Stevenson's murder."

Officer Chadwick's expression was unchanged. "Go on."

Addie cleared her throat and pressed her knees together. "Have you ever heard of the Gap Lake Mystery series? They're books." Addie pulled her copy out of her purse and slid it over the desk.

Chadwick nodded slowly. "I've heard of these. Not really up my alley." She dropped her head and leaned in. "Don't tell anyone, but I'm kind of a romance gal."

Addie felt herself flush and then Chadwick let out a low chuckle. "What? You thought I was a guns and ammo girl? Some of us in blue have a heart."

She tried to smile, tried to feel light, but everything weighed heavily on her. "I heard someone on the news say Lydia's killer might be a copycat."

Officer Chadwick raised a single eyebrow, but nothing else about her expression changed. Addie cleared her throat, wrung her hands. "If so, the copycat is basing his kills on these novels."

A slight head bob from Chadwick.

"And I think that person is contacting me."

Now Chadwick narrowed her eyes. "What exactly do you mean?"

Addie pulled out the pages she had printed up and slid them

across the Formica table. "This is everything. And…he's…" she looked over both shoulders, feeling both ridiculous and paranoid. She was in a police station; she should feel safe. But she didn't.

"He said he's watching me. I said I was going to the police and—"

"Addison?"

Addie turned in the hard metal chair, her eyes meeting Chief Garcia's.

"Mrs., um, Chief Garcia. How's Maya?"

The chief nodded. "She's going to be fine. May I ask what you're doing here?"

Addie cleared her throat again even though it felt raw. "I think I have information about Lydia's death and maybe about who hit Maya." She licked her lips and dropped her eyes. "And why."

Chief Garcia's eyes were sharp, but she offered Addie a small smile. "Thank you, Officer Chadwick. I can take over from here. Addie, why don't you come to my office?"

Addie smiled to Chadwick and trailed behind Chief Garcia, who walked at a fast clip, her boots sharp thumps on the scuffed linoleum. She took a sharp turn into her office and gestured for Addie to come in. Addie started, stopped.

Detective Garcia was sitting there, staring at Addie.

THIRTY-SEVEN

"Hi, Mr.…Detective…Garcia."

He nodded, his lips pressed in a hard, bloodless line.

"Can I get you something to drink?"

Addie stood there, dumbfounded. It was a stupid question but she had no idea how to answer. The Garcias seemed to be studying her, watching her every move. *Would a guilty person want a drink?*

"Um, no, I'm okay."

"How about you have a seat then?" Chief Garcia gestured to a chair and the detective pulled it out for Addie. She sat down, arranging the papers on her lap, their edges cool and damp from her sweating palms.

"Why don't you tell us why you're here, Addison?"

She licked her lips, then licked them again. "Uh, well it's about Lydia. Lydia Stevenson? You know we—"

"You found the body. Yes, we know."

The body.

Again that word struck Addie, hit hard at her soul. Lydia Stevenson was simply "the body" now.

Addie swallowed again, wishing she had asked for that glass of water. "Well, her death kind of mimics these books that everyone is reading…"

"The Gap Lake mystery series. We're aware," said Chief Garcia.

Addie felt her eyes go round. "So you know that it looks like a copycat—"

"That's one theory," Detective Garcia said. "Not a great one."

Addie blinked. "What?"

"Addison, the Gap Lake mysteries are a series written for teens. The murders aren't realistic, and not done well enough to pull off in real life."

Addie's tongue felt heavy in her mouth. "So you don't think—"

"Why are you here, Addison?"

She spread the pages on Chief Garcia's desk. "I've been talking to someone who says they are R. J. Rosen, the author of the books. Not talking…emailing and text messaging mostly. The first message said there was going to be a 'surprise'"—she made air quotes—"for me after I posted the first story. The only surprise that came up was Lydia Stevenson."

Addie waited for Chief Garcia and Detective Garcia to say something, to react. They didn't.

"I know it doesn't sound like much, but then he wanted me to post something else—and then when I didn't, he said I'd be sorry."

"Is that it?" the detective asked.

Addie shook her head. "No. He said I would be sorry and then someone hit Maya with their car. She was wearing my jacket." Addie was crying now, her nose running, hiccupping as she tried to speak. "Don't you see? I'm the reason Maya got hit and I might be the reason Lydia died and remember the photos I told you about? The ones from my blog?"

Chief Garcia came around her desk and engulfed Addie in a hug. "Honey, none of this is your fault."

The detective leaned forward, his jaw still set. "None of this is about you, Addie."

She blinked. "I just…I…"

He tilted his head. "Are you still talking to R. J. Rosen now?"

Addie sniffed and shook her head. "I told him I didn't want him to contact me anymore. I said I was going to the police."

"And did he respond?"

"He said things were going to get worse for me."

Detective Garcia gathered Addie's pages up with a swipe of his big hand. He straightened them and gave her a tight, unamused smile. "We'll look into these emails and we'll look into this R. J. Rosen character."

"Thank you," Addie said. "Thank you." She looked from the detective to the chief. "I'm so, so sorry about Maya."

Chief Garcia put her hand gently on Addie's shoulder. "Thank you for that, but Maya's going to be just fine. As a matter of fact, she's a little too fine. The doctors want us to keep her home for the rest of the week."

Addie tried to smile. "I bet she loves that."

"She's already commandeered the downstairs couch and built a wall out of junk food. It's possible she thinks sugar rebuilds broken bones."

* * *

Addie zipped her coat up to her chin, crossing the police station parking lot and stepping onto the sidewalk. Her father was on his way to pick her up, but Addie decided not to mention her stop at the police department. She told him she was at the coffee shop across the street and when she pushed the button, waiting for the light to change, she saw the car from the corner of her eye. Navy blue, parked in the police station lot. There was someone in the front seat but the sun visor was down, and the breaking twilight blacked out the whole front window.

Addie's heartbeat ratcheted up the second the driver flicked on his lights and started the engine. Hairs pricked at the back of her neck and she lost her breath when she heard the crunch of tires spitting out gravel.

"Oh God." She spun around, cornered. If she stepped back into the police station parking lot the car had a clear shot at her. If she stayed where she was—the car still had a clear shot.

Addie flapped her hands, willing herself not to cry. "I don't even know what kind of car that is," she muttered to herself. "I don't even know—"

The car shot out of the lot and Addie darted across the street. Horns blared. Tires screeched. She cleared the street and the curb, and she had her hand on the knob of the coffeehouse when someone grabbed her from behind.

THIRTY-EIGHT

"No!" Addie's scream was primitive, guttural. She clamped her eyes shut, her hand sliding off the doorknob as her attacker pinned her against his chest, swept her feet off the ground.

"Addie, Addie, baby, it's okay, it's me. It's your dad."

She stopped struggling, letting his deep voice wash over her. Her heart still slammed against her ribs, her mind spinning, not letting her relax, not letting her breathe.

"Addie."

Morton Gaines steadied Addie on her feet, turned her around to face him. His hands were soft, his lips pulled into a worried line.

"What's happened, hon? You darted into the street. You ran into oncoming traffic."

Addie could barely hear for the rush of blood in her ears. She shook her head slowly, not trusting herself to talk. Her father wrapped his arms around her, and Addie slumped against him, loving the calming steady *thrum* of his heart. She didn't know that she was crying, but tears were spilling over her cheeks, her whole body pulsing with adrenaline.

"I think I'm…I just…I don't know anymore, Dad."

Addie's father slung his arm around her shoulders, gathering her to him and helping her walk. He opened the passenger side door and helped Addie in, leaning over to buckle her belt. By the time he got into the driver's side and turned the key, Addie was spent. She was slumped, every bit of energy leaving her body. The anxiety she usually felt while riding with her father was sapped; her legs felt heavy, her body felt weak. She leaned forward and rested her head on the dash, barely registering when the navy blue Dodge pulled out from behind them and passed.

* * *

Addie awoke with a start the next morning. The sun was streaking through the windows, warm slashes across her face. If she just kept her eyes closed she could hover for a few more minutes in this half sleep, in this calm state where Lydia wasn't dead, R. J. Rosen wasn't contacting her, and she was back to being a closeted bookworm that no one paid any attention to.

She rolled over onto her side and dialed Maya, counting the rings until, "Hello?"

"Maya, you sound great!"

"That's good, because I feel crappy."

"Does it hurt much?"

Addie heard Maya shift on her mattress on her end of the phone. "Sort of. But the really crappy thing is the doctors told my dad I should try to walk and do these stupid exercises. He showed up at the foot of my bed in sweatpants and a whistle this morning."

"He did not!"

"No, he didn't. But close. He brought donuts and made me go downstairs to get mine. Like a freaking animal."

Addie laughed, the action feeling so foreign but so good.

"How you doing, Adds?"

Addie wanted to tell Maya that she had gone to the police station. She wanted to tell her about the car in the parking lot, but something nagged at her. She didn't want to dump on her donut-foraging best friend. "I'm okay."

"No, you're not."

"Why do you say that?"

"Because I know you better than you know you. Because I know that you're still in bed and Addison Gaines is all 'up with the crows' or whatever like her dad. So if you're still in bed…"

Addie kicked off the covers and stood up. "You're wrong, I'm actually up."

"Prove it."

Addie snapped a selfie and shot it to Maya.

Maya yawned. "That's a terrible selfie. Want to hang out today?"

"I can't. Work."

"I can't believe you can go in to work when I've been through such trauma."

"I'll manage. But I'll call you later, okay?"

THIRTY-NINE

"I'm glad you're here," Ella said when Addie walked into the store that evening. "The Neanderthal vandals have struck again." She jutted her chin toward the three mannequins at the front of the store.

Addie rolled her eyes. Two of the mannequins were dressed in Bereman's attire and posed in their factory-direct, supermodel stances. The third had her pants pulled around her skinny white ankles and her blouse scarfed around her neck. She was headless and "Class of 2020 RULES" was scrawled in Sharpie or eyeliner across her torso and down her arms, which had been yanked off and reattached to reach to the ceiling.

"When did that happen?"

"Somewhere between the afternoon rush and the late afternoon rush."

"We're a boutique; we don't have rushes."

Ella crossed her arms in front of her chest. "So you're saying that my enormous sale of one bangle each to seven different teenagers was a distraction technique?"

"Class of 2020 rules."

"Can you move her please? My back is still messed up. Can't lift anything heavier than this pen." Ella demonstrated with a blue ballpoint. "And I was supposed to be off exactly nine minutes ago."

Addie sighed. "With a commission haul from the bangles, I'd expect you to be halfway to the Bahamas by now. I hate going to the storeroom."

"I think you're going to be okay."

Addie nodded. "Fine."

She cut through the racks of clothing and found the offending mannequin, throwing her arms around its narrow waist and dragging it backward. Even headless, the thing was a good foot taller than she was, and Addie had to wrestle it through the store.

"You'd think they'd get smart and put mannequins on wheels, you know?" she said to Ella. Ella didn't answer and Addie shrugged, sighing when she got to the double doors that led to the storeroom.

She hated the storeroom.

Everyone did. Even in broad daylight it was creepy, a weird, vast room shoulder to shoulder with naked mannequins that for some reason, Mr. Bereman refused to throw away. The mannequins were in all manner of disrepair: headless, armless, the occasional torso or disembodied head stacked on shelves or tossed in baskets.

Addie had the padlock in one hand and was throwing the lock on the bolt when she heard the tinkle of bells from the front door. She craned her head to see Ella's chest rise with a heaving sigh. Customers. If she was going to make Addie drag Ms. Headless to Mannequinland, Ella would just have to handle them herself.

She heard Ella's forced cheery voice, "Hello, welcome to

Bereman's. Can I help you find something?" before she wrestled the defiled mannequin into the storeroom, stopping to grope for the light switch. Addie waited a beat for the LED light to go from dusty yellow to bright and when it did, she bit her bottom lip.

"They're fake," she said out loud. "Totally fake."

The sea of dead-faced mannequins reaching out for her was like a mini scene from *The Walking Dead*: a thousand zombies with outstretched arms. She shuddered, doing her best to work her mannequin into the fold.

"There you go, lady. You're with all your little mannequin friends." She paused, knowing that per Bereman's policy she was supposed to take the clothes off the mannequin and fill out the stupid little paper telling management why that particular mannequin was being retired. She glanced at the thing, words scrawled down the torso, and muttered, "Isn't it obvious?" But still, Addie pulled off the mannequin's blouse and shorts, then grabbed a pencil and paper. She started to write but paused, certain somehow that all those dead eyes were watching her, studying her, the mannequins ready to pounce.

"No offense to all of you creepy bastards, but I'm going to do this out there." Addie had one hand on the light switch and the other on the door frame when the first scent of smoke hit her nose. She sneezed.

"Ella, are you smok—" The door wouldn't move.

Addie's skin prickled with a wash of wet heat. She swallowed hard and took a deep breath. The door often stuck. The dead bolt, even when unlocked, almost always caught. Addie licked her lips, trying to steel herself.

"It always catches. Just jiggle the handle."

She did that but nothing happened.

The smoke smell started to get a little stronger and Addie coughed. "Ella? Ella!"

Panic started to rise in her chest. Addie threw her shoulder against the door, her body weight hitting square with an impressive thud, but the door didn't budge. Tears pricked at the backs of her eyes.

"Calm down, calm down. Take a deep breath." Addie fanned her face and opened her mouth, then clamped a hand over it. Smoke licked tiny waves under the small gap at the bottom of the door.

The fire alarm cut through the silence in the storeroom, an ear-splitting screech that shook the windows and throbbed through Addie's skull.

A big, racking sob rose and broke in her chest, and Addie was crying as she yanked on the storeroom door, kicked it, beat it with her fists.

"Help me, help me!"

She turned, looking for anything to pound against the door, anything to boost her high enough to scratch at the little window on the door, but there was nothing but the mannequins, the disembodied heads, the blank eyes staring back at her. Addie clawed for the door as the licks of smoke turned into bellows, as the fire alarm droned.

"I'm in here!" she screamed, her voice caught on the sputter and click of the overhead sprinklers before they released a torrent of icy cold silencing water. It pounded on her head and rolled into her eyes and Addie's vision was blurred, first by the tears, then by the water. "Help," she whispered, sinking to her knees.

She was going to die.

She was going to burn to death or drown to death surrounded by a horde of stupid mannequins.

Follow-through is important. R. J. Rosen's words flashed before her eyes. *Do what I say or else.*

No.

Addie thought of Jordan fighting, clawing at her killer, desperate to save her own life.

The story is just getting good.

She yanked her T-shirt up over her nose and mouth, squinted against the water and wet smoke and felt along the sodden carpet, shoving into mannequin legs with her shoulders. She would get out of there. The killer couldn't win.

There wasn't enough room to crawl so Addie crouched, her thighs screaming with the effort. She knew there was an outside door at the back of the storeroom. If she could just make it there…

The fire alarm droned. The sprinklers kept up their incessant drip, drops of water pounding her skull and thudding through her brain.

I'm going to get out of here.

The smell of smoke was everywhere, the black plumes surrounding her head, half-pounded out by the splashes of water. Addie pushed past one body after another and they started to tumble like a row of dominoes, body after body falling forward, arms outstretched, rigor mortis fingers pointing at her, blank eyes somehow accusing.

You did this, they seemed to be saying. *You did this to Lydia, and you did this to yourself.*

"No, no…" Addie's vision seemed to fish-eye and wobble; a thousand eyes staring at her. Her breath was strangled, a deep ache in her throat. Her head felt light, then impossibly heavy.

It was the smoke.

She tried not to breathe, tried not to think that the mannequins were moving now, slow, plodding steps toward her with a low, droning, accusing moan. Everyone in town thought that she brought a murderer into their midst. Everyone in town was right.

She stopped moving, stopped trying to fight. The mannequins were an army, were Hawthorne High students, were faces she recognized: Lydia. Spencer. Colton. Maya.

"No," she muttered, her lips puckered and parched with the heat. "I didn't. I didn't mean to…"

The fire bell stopped and the water from the sprinklers lightened to a gentle trickle but there was a crashing, a pounding. Addie's heart. Her bones as the army crashed in on her, the mannequins reached and pointed and taunted and gnawed.

And then there was silence.

FORTY

The beeping was incessant. It kept going, loud, insistent, even as Addie gritted her teeth and clenched her eyes shut harder, doing her best to burrow under her covers to drown the sound out.

"She's stirring."

"I think she's waking up."

Addie could hear the voices somewhere in the distance, shrouded in sleep or somehow underwater. Was she in Gap Lake? In between the beeps she could almost hear the lap of the lake against the shore and she was so warm, her bare shoulders lolling into the sand, the sun beating down on her face.

"Addie?"

It sounded like Declan Levy. Or at least, it sounded like the gravelly voice she made up for him in her head. That was it. She was in Gap Lake on junior cut day, lying in the sand and Declan was looking over her, casting a cool shadow over her neck and forearms.

But Gap Lake wasn't real.

Declan Levy wasn't real.

And the beeping…

She tried to move, tried to move an arm or wriggle a finger but she was a thousand pounds, weighted down. There was pressure on her chest. A pounding in her temples. She tried to lick her lips, but there was not a drop of moisture left in her body and her throat was ripped raw.

Lydia's hands were on both sides of Addie's face, her fingernails thin and wet digging into Addie's cheeks. Her eyes were bright, wide, but milky somehow and her words were garbled, drowned out by the beeping.

"She's coming around!"

Addie gasped, clawing her own chest, feeling the heat of torn skin as her fingernails dug into her flesh.

"Where am I?"

The light was blindingly white and she wasn't weighted down anymore—she was floating, faces swirling around her.

A light in her eye.

"She's going to be okay?"

"What is…where am…?"

"She's trying to talk. Can we take off the oxygen mask?"

Addie's eyes widened at the giant hand that came for her, that removed the gag from her mouth. She sucked in a great lungful of air, the oxygen ripping holes in her already torn throat, cutting through her lungs like razor blades. The tears poured over her cheeks.

"Where am I?"

"You're safe, sweetheart…you're safe, baby." Her father stood near her shoulder, his voice soothing but too slow, his head cocked as he stared at her with eyes riddled with terror. He stroked her hand and Addie realized hers was ice cold.

"Where—"

"In the hospital."

"I'll let you two talk." The voice she thought was Declan Levy's belonged to an older man in a long white coat. "Ma'am?"

Addie craned her head. "Maya?"

Maya was by her feet, a hand each on Addie's big toes. "Thank God, you're awake. I would have had to kill you if you died."

"Give us a minute?" Morton said, eyes toward Maya.

Maya gave a curt nod and shook Addie's right toe. "I'll be back as soon as they let me."

"Dad, what's going on?" Addie asked once Maya and the doctor left.

"Do you remember anything?"

Addie scanned the room, her eyes skipping over the sterile white everything, taking in the IV taped to her arm, the needle buried in the back of her hand. Her stomach lurched and she thought of Lydia, of her cold hands on her face. "Did it have something to do with Lydia Stevenson?"

Her father looked taken aback. "Oh, honey, no, I don't think so. You were in a fire, remember? At the store. You were in the storeroom when they found you."

Addie tried to think back but the beeping and the ache that was forming behind her eyes were making it hard. She remembered hands, so many hands reaching for her and the cold, accusing eyes…

"The mannequins."

Morton nodded. "Yes, the storeroom. You were passed out."

"I was locked in."

He started. "What?"

"I was locked in the storeroom. Sometimes the lock sticks but…I couldn't get out and Ella—where's Ella? Oh my God, Dad, is she okay?"

Mr. Gaines blinked. "Ella's fine. She was the one who called in the fire. She ran out for a second because she thought she saw the kids who had vandalized some mannequins, and when she came back, she saw the smoke and called it in. Thank God she did."

Addie shook her head slowly, the effort monumental, the pain just as bad. She pressed her fingertips to her temples to get the incessant drumbeat to stop. She tried to think. There was something else, something else hanging on the edge of her peripheral. "Voices. There were other voices."

Her father nodded slowly. "They were probably customers."

Addie could feel a lick of heat low in her gut. He was patronizing her. "Yeah, but Ella was there and there were customers so how…where…what happened to the store?"

Morton Gaines rubbed his palms on his jeans, paced the length of Addie's bed. "The police aren't saying much, but they think the fire looked suspicious."

"Is the store still there? I mean, did it…did it burn down or anything?"

"There's a significant amount of damage. We were just so lucky that the fire alarm was working and the fire department was able to get to you in time. If not…if…I don't know what I would have done—" Morton turned to Addie, his eyes glossy. He sniffed and took both of her hands, squeezing tightly. "I don't even want to think about it."

Addie nodded, a lump forming in her own throat. She could have died.

The fire looked suspicious…

"Do they think someone set the fire?"

Morton paused for a beat. He licked his lips, looked away.

"Dad?"

"It's an old building, Addie. The wiring was probably faulty. I don't think anyone would intentionally set a fire like that."

Addie wasn't so sure.

It's only going to get worse for you.

FORTY-ONE

Mr. Gaines pulled into the driveway and sped around the car, pulling open the passenger side door for his daughter.

"I'm fine, Dad," Addie said, but she was smiling, enjoying her father fawning over her, his full attention hers.

"Let's just get you set up in the living room. Do you want pizza? We can order pizza, anything you want."

"No." Addie swung her head. "I'm fine. I'm not even hungry."

A *ping* from her cell phone made Addie's whole body stiffen, her blood run cold.

"Oh jeez," her father said, a deep frown on his face. "We left your prescription." He raised his brows. "Back in the car or do you want to wait here?"

"I wouldn't hate a milkshake with those pills." Addie smiled.

He father yanked open his car door and grinned. "You got it. Twenty minutes, tops. Go inside and relax. If Louisa isn't still there, I'm sure she's stocked the entire place with snacks and meals." He swallowed, his eyes covered with a slight mist. "I was really worried about you, Addison. When I got that call…"

Addie nodded sharply, not wanting to cry. "It's okay, Dad."

She let herself into the house, shrugging out of her jacket and going straight to the junk drawer. She fished out a pair of scissors, then cut the hospital band from her wrist, watching the thing sail to the floor.

Someone had really tried to hurt her.

The realization sent a shock wave through her. Addie sunk into a dining room chair, holding her head in her hands. Suddenly, her house felt cavernous and dark. She spun in her chair, feeling eyes all over her.

I've been watching you...

No. It was over. She had gone to the police, she had turned over the emails—and someone had tried to singe her to a crisp.

But she had survived.

She was grinning until she remembered that there was an active murder investigation going on in her town. She startled when she heard a door slam in the other room.

Her heart started to thud, beating the breath out of her chest. "Uh-uh," she muttered to herself. "Hello?" It was weak, strangled. She didn't want to be heard.

She didn't want someone to answer back.

Addie gripped the stairway banister, resting her foot on the first step. She cocked her head, listening.

Someone's heart was beating. Someone's breath was a thunderous roar.

"It's me. It's me! I'm freaking myself the crap out. Everything is fine. There is no one in my house and doors slammed because windows were open and wind rushed and stuff." She glanced out the kitchen window, hoping for a gust or a hurricane, but the leaves on the birch trees weren't moving at all. The night was solid, still. Deathly quiet.

She grabbed her cell phone from her back pocket, speed dialed Maya. "Pick up, pick up!"

"Maya's Psychic Services. Your loss is my gain. Are you home?"

"I thought you were a psychic?"

"My powers tell me this is Addison Gaines calling to tell me about something creepy or murderous."

Addie groaned. "Your psychic powers have discovered caller ID." She bit her bottom lip. "I just need to talk. I'm freaking out and my dad went to get my meds. He'll be home in like twenty minutes."

"Do you want me to come too? I can kick down doors, clear the place? Pretty sure I have pepper spray in my Prada bag."

"That Prada bag is mine. Just stay on the phone, okay?"

"I'll come over but it's going to take me about a half hour, what with you living in Boondockville and me driving a horse and buggy."

"You drive a Honda."

"And you could be driving a vintage Mustang."

Addie's stomach knotted. "Shut up. Just stay on the phone. I'm going to investigate."

"Do you have a Maglite and a Sig Sauer?"

Addie paused on the third stair. "I don't know what either of those things are."

"A flashlight and a gun."

"I have a cell phone and the daughter of two cops on standby."

"Good enough." Maya paused. "Are you really worried though? Maybe you should just wait for your dad outside. Or go over to Colton's."

"I think I'm just being a little freaky."

"Ooh." Addie could practically hear the waggle in Maya's voice.

"Not in a gross way."

"Someone tried to light you on fire, Addie. It's okay to be freaked out."

"But I was feeling fine five minutes ago."

"Addie, Colton is right next door. You're fine, girl. I promise. There is no boogeyman."

Addie opened the door to her father's room and poked her head in. The room was pristine, just as Louisa left it: vacuum lines in the carpet. Hospital corners on the bed. The mirrors and marble counters glittering in the bathroom.

"Well, he's not sleeping in Papa Bear's bed."

"I'm pretty sure you're okay."

Addie crossed the hall to her own room, doing a cursory check in the closet. She shifted the basket of clean laundry on the window seat, lifted the dust ruffle on the bed with her sneakered foot. "Pretty sure I'm okay too, except for the dust bunnies under my bed."

"Dust bunnies?" Maya snorted. "What are you, a hundred?"

She rolled her eyes, poked her head in the bathroom. The shower curtain was pulled, her bathrobe on the back of the door. "Okay, I was officially being lame."

"So you're not about to die?"

"Not tonight, sorry to disappoint. Thanks anyway, though. I think I'm going to take a shower."

"I knew you were going to say that."

"Of course you did."

Addie swiped off her phone and tossed it on the counter, then pulled her shirt over her head. She shimmied out of her pants and took the rest of her clothes off, then grabbed a towel from the basket. She turned on the bathroom faucet and yanked the curtain.

Her heart gave a panicked double thump.

Heat pricked out along her spine.

Footprints.

Standing at the back of her tub, a pair of dirty boot prints. Someone had been in her house. Someone had been in her shower.

FORTY-TWO

"Oh my God!"

"Addie? Honey? Are you okay?"

Addie heard the front door creak open and swing shut. She heard the lock drop as she thundered down the stairs, towel wrapped around her chest. "There was someone in my shower."

"What? Addison—"

"Dad, I'm serious. We have to get out of here. We have to call Maya's parents. Whoever set the fire probably followed me home, Dad, he—"

"Addie, wait." Morton Gaines pushed Addie behind him. "Your upstairs shower?"

"Yes, Dad, what are you doing?"

"I'm going to go check."

"Dad, no!"

A sob caught in Addie's throat. Tears lined up on her lower lashes. Addie's father turned to face her, resting his hands on her shoulders. "You've been through a really traumatic couple of weeks, honey. You're just jumpy."

Anger curled over the fear in Addie's gut. "Jumpy? Dad, I know what I saw. I'll show you."

She followed her father up the stairs and into her bedroom. The faucet was still on full bore, steam filling the bathroom. Addie yanked back the shower curtain, pointing. "See? There!"

Morton Gaines leaned over and turned off the water, eyes sweeping across the pristine white porcelain. "There's nothing there, hon."

Addie blinked, searching the tub.

"I know what I saw. They were right there! Two boot prints. Big ones. They were right there."

"Honey, there's nothing there. Look, why don't you take the medication and lay down? The doctor said it will help you relax—"

"The steam! The steam and the water! They're gone because of the steam, but they were there, I promise you! I promise, Dad, you've got to believe me."

Mr. Gaines stood up and gathered Addie in a hug, kissing her forehead. He pulled her robe from the back of the bathroom door and draped it over her shoulders, then filled a glass with water. He poured a single pill from the little orange container into the palm of his hand and held it out with Addie.

"This will help you calm down."

Addie sniffed, salt tears rolling over her cheeks. "I'm not crazy."

"I know you're not, sweetie. You're just tired. It's been a long day."

Addie shook her head. "You're never around, Dad. You don't understand. You don't know what's been going on."

Morton Gaines's eyes went to the pill in the palm of his hand, his other hand holding the water out to his daughter. "You'll feel better, okay? You'll sleep tonight and tomorrow we can figure this whole thing out. I'm just going to go in for a few hours and get my stuff, then I'll work from home the rest of the week. Louisa—"

Addie stamped her bare foot. "No! Not Louisa! I'm tired of being your second thought, Dad. Someone tried to kill me tonight! Someone has been harassing me for weeks!"

Her father didn't say anything, his hazel eyes clear and wide. "You just need to rest, Addie."

Addie swallowed the pill and shut the door on her father, shrugging into a nightshirt and sliding into bed. She didn't want to think. She didn't want to dream. Her eyes closed just as she saw her curtains flutter against her open window. The air sucked them in and out, in and out. If Addie hadn't been so tired, so would have realized that someone had removed the screen from her window.

* * *

Addie slept like the dead, waking up past eleven the following morning. There were four messages on her phone. She thumbed through the first three—Maya, checking in; Louisa, saying she was on her way; her father, saying he would be home by two. There was another one from Louisa, but Addie didn't listen to it.

She had something she wanted to do.

She sat in front of her computer, lips pursed, anger coursing through her.

"Please stop contacting me," she typed. "This isn't funny anymore. I've gone to the police."

She sucked in a shaky breath and closed her eyes when she hit Send. She didn't know what she expected: her laptop to explode, R. J. Rosen to come through the screen to strangle her, her cell phone to start pinging with a waterfall of horrific images, but none of it happened. There was nothing but silence—and that was unnerving. Her entire house seemed to be holding its breath and Addie realized she was holding hers too. She let out a whoosh of air and her laptop pinged.

MAILERDAEMON: Your message could not be sent.

Addie tried to read the gobbledygook in the message portion of the email—something about the address not found and the server no longer trying. She hit Send a second time, and this time the message bounced back immediately.

FORTY-THREE

Addie went for her phone, squealing when it rang in her hand.

"Hello?"

"Addie, this is Chief Garcia."

She nodded, unsure she could form words.

"Are you there, dear?"

"Yes." It was barely a whisper.

"We're going to need you to come down to the station."

"I…there's no one home. My…Louisa is supposed to be here soon and my dad will be here in a few hours but…is there something wrong?"

Chief Garcia paused dramatically and Addie's heart started to thump. "We've been going over the emails, the ones you said came from the author R. J. Rosen?"

"Yeah, I just tried to—"

"Addie, I don't know what you're trying to pull, but the charade is up."

"What? What are you talking about?"

"We traced the IP address. We know where the emails are coming from, Addison. We know they're coming from you."

Addie's blood ran cold. "What do you mean? Someone sent them—"

"Someone sent them from your computer, Addison. You know it's a crime to hinder an investigation."

"I didn't—I didn't." Addie shook her head, the tears starting to fall again. "I didn't send the emails to myself! I didn't!"

"They came from your computer, Addison. We can prove it. Please have your father drive you down here at your earliest convenience."

The click on the other end of the phone was deafening.

Addie immediately dialed her father. For once, he picked up on the first ring. "Everything okay, hon? Is Louisa taking good care of you?"

"She's not here yet. Are you coming home soon?"

"Half hour, tops. Everything okay?"

Addie bit her lip. "No. Please just hurry, okay?"

Still shaking, Addie padded down the stairs, her heartbeat only slowing to a normal pace when she heard Louisa's keys in the door. She laid her cell phone on the banister and craned her neck.

"Hello?" she called toward the foyer.

Then she heard the chuckle. It was slightly off, a forced laugh coming from the kitchen.

Dad?

Heat pricked at the back of Addie's neck but she shrugged it off, stopping short when she stepped into the kitchen. The lights were off, curtains drawn, everything cast in shadow. She went for the light switch.

"I didn't know people actually did that in real life."

Addie's stomach dropped, but she forced her fingers to find the light switch.

"Spencer?"

"Really, I thought that was just a stupid horror movie thing, you know? Pretty young ingénue yells out, 'hello?' signaling to the killer exactly where she is." He shook his head.

"What are you talking…and how did you get in here?"

Spencer looked up, weirdly shocked to see Addie standing there in front of him in her own kitchen. Then he grinned, a beaming, tooth-bared grin that in the past made Addie's knees weak.

But today, it was chilling, slightly off.

He dangled Addie's spare keys in front of his nose, still grinning. "Lose something?"

Addie scratched her neck. "Those are mine."

"I know."

She held out her hand. Spencer stared at her palm but made no move to hand the keys over.

"Can I have them, please?"

He pressed his lips together, cocked his head, and studied the keys. "So the young ingénue thinks that asking nicely will make everything okay."

"Spencer, I want my keys. I'm just asking for you to give them back and…you don't have to leave, we could just hang out or something. My housekeeper will be here in a few minutes. She could make us something to eat." Addie shifted her weight, a strange mix of anxiety and hope thrumming through her.

"Do you think this is a date?"

"What? What are you—"

"Do you think this is a social call, Addie?"

Addie reached for her keys and Spencer snatched them back, slammed them on the table. His eyes went sharp and hard.

"I think you should leave. Give me my keys and go. Please."

Spencer blinked, dragged his tongue over his lower lip, and settled into a slow, comfortable smile. He looked like regular Spencer, the guy from school with the adorable half smile. But his voice was lower than Addie was used to.

"This isn't a social call." He bit off his words.

Addie held her hands up. "Okay, Spencer. Look, Louisa and my dad are going to be here—"

"Louisa's not going to make it."

Addie blinked. "What?"

Spencer rubbed his stomach and shook his head sadly. "She ate something that she shouldn't have."

"What are you—"

"Rat poison."

Addie felt like someone struck her in the gut. "What are you talking about?"

Spencer's eyes went wide. "Oh, don't worry. She's not going to die! She just ate a little bit." He held his thumb and forefinger apart a quarter inch. "Doesn't take much to knock someone out for a couple of days. Didn't you get her message?"

"Did you poison Louisa?"

Spencer didn't answer. His eyes were fixed on hers. She held his gaze, her hand darting for the keys.

He clamped a hand over her wrist, yanking her toward him so her hip dug into the edge of the table, her ribs crushing against the pushed-in chair.

"Spencer, what the—"

His voice was a serpentine whisper. *"It was a calm, easy day in Gap Lake. The tourists were baking in the sun, sucking down Slurpees and ice creams, but Jordan was fighting for her life."*

Addie stopped struggling.

Spencer still held Addie against him, his breath hot on her cheek. "Do you know what it feels like to fight for your life?"

Addie sucked in a breath, tried to steel herself. This was her friend, Spencer. This was a high school kid who only stood a few inches taller than she did. "No, I don't."

"You write about it."

"I write fiction."

"It looks terrible. When someone is taking their last breath? Is struggling to live?" He blew out a sigh and shook his head, his fingers digging into Addie's forearm. "You know the look. Eyes, frozen in fear. Mouth opened, but nothing coming out. Like, like—"

"A silent scream."

Spencer pumped his head and Addie could see his cheek rise. He was smiling. "Yeah, yeah, that's exactly it. You know what I'm talking about."

Addie slowly licked her chapped lips. "Because I'm a good writer."

"No!" Spencer yelled, tightening up on Addie's wrist and twisting it ever so slightly. A needle of pain shot up her forearm, a lightning bolt that exploded on her shoulder. She winced.

There was fury in Spencer's eyes. His nostrils flared and Addie could feel his breath coming in short, hot bursts.

"Spencer. Let. Me. Go."

He flicked a tongue over his bottom lip, his teeth showing as his lips inched up into a too-pleased grin.

"Don't you want to be with me, Addie?"

FORTY-FOUR

His voice was hot tar. Addie's eyes swept the kitchen table, her hand circling a wooden pepper grinder. Spencer saw it too, amusement in his eyes. The edge of his lips quirked up until Addie cracked the grinder against his temple. Wood clacked against flesh and Spencer's smile turned into a scowl. His eyebrow was cracked open, a tiny slice that bubbled with blood.

"Bitch!"

He released Addie, gingerly pressing his hand against his forehead and cheek. Addie turned, her sneakers *eek*ing on the linoleum.

Spencer sent a kitchen chair crashing into her. It caught her mid-thigh and her knees buckled; she tripped over her own feet and slammed chest-first to the ground, letting out an inelegant "Oof!"

She tried to struggle, tried to scream, but her breath was gone and Spencer stomped a foot in the middle of her back, stepping on her, gathering the chair. Addie heaved; her ribs ached against the tiled floor, her back sagged under Spencer's weight. He stepped off and kicked her so she was laying on her back. Addie tried to sit up, tried to move, but Spencer caged her with the legs of the chair.

"Spencer, please—" Her voice was soft, choked.

He slid down, backward, on the seat of the chair, arms slung over the back, and grinned. "You shouldn't have done that, Addie."

She was pinned, arms akimbo, completely stuck. And then she saw the glint of the knife. Spencer was looking at it too, the thing silver and shiny in his hand, glaring with hints of sunlight.

"I can't wait to kill you."

"No…Spencer, why? Why? What did I ever do to you?"

Spencer glared down at her, his face pulsating with rage; a mask of sinister red. "You could have stopped him," he said slowly, biting off each word. "You should have stopped him."

"What are you—"

"Your dad."

"I have no idea what you're talking about."

"You know why I had to hide in the closet whenever my dad came home?"

"He drinks, Spencer." Addie tried to shrug him off. "You told me he drinks. It's okay, my dad does too."

"Oh, that's right, he does. He drinks and plows into a market full of people."

A sob lodged in Addie's chest. "No one got hurt." It sounded like a weak and stupid excuse and Spencer raged, tightening his grip.

"That's right! No one got hurt, and your dad walked home and got to sleep in his bed that night. Because your daddy's rich, so he suffers no consequences."

"Please, Spencer, if you need to talk, we could talk about this. We could go somewhere."

"How about to my house?"

Addie raised her hands, palms up. "Sure, okay, of course. Wherever you want."

His eyes narrowed. His nostrils flared again and that breathing: hard, fast, hot, started again. "I don't have a house anymore. Your rich daddy took it."

Addie shook her head, her hair snapping and breaking under the legs of the chair. "No. No, he didn't."

"My dad invested everything and your dad just took it. Everything." He licked his lips, his teeth bared. "Everything but the vodka bottles."

"I'm sorry, Spencer, I didn't know. The market was bad for everyone, I guess. It was—"

"Just business?" He cocked his head. "That's what your dad said too. And my dad started drinking. And my mom took off because she couldn't deal with it anymore. And she was going to come back for me, but you know what? She didn't. And you! You get to live here"—he threw out his arms—"in this fucking castle where nothing bad ever happens because you're Morton Gaines's daughter. And if he bankrupts people it doesn't matter. And if he drives drunk and mows down eighteen rows of cabbage, it doesn't matter!"

"I'm so, so sorry, Spencer."

"Are you? 'Cause your dad rolls out a little tipsy and gets a slap on the wrist. My dad does and he loses his job. His license. Our house."

"I didn't know."

Spencer paused, his breath still coming in ragged gasps and

Addie thought he was softening, listening. She watched the fingers on his hand open and close over the hilt of the knife.

"You. Should. Have. Stopped. Him!" Spencer sliced with each word, the point of the blade coming within a hairsbreadth of Addie's chest.

"I live in a fucking motel, Addie, while you live here in this goddamn mansion." Spencer lurched over the chair's back. "My mom walked out because my dad is a fucking mess! He's a mess because your dad took everything he had and he came home to his precious fucking Goody Two-shoes daughter and got to live his life. Home fucking free." He was spitting, chewing on the words. His eyes were wild, brown-black, and Addie was terrified, unable to move even as bits of spit struck her lips and cheeks.

"He never suffered. He never had to know suffering. But…" Spencer's eyes cut to the knife, one finger running the length of the blade and drawing a pristine red thread of blood. He smiled once again, and Addie wondered how she never noticed how maniacal that smile was. "But…" Spencer sucked his bloody finger and grinned again, this time his teeth stained a haunting pink. He pinned Addie with those wild eyes and spat, blood-tinged saliva spraying all over her chin and neck. "Now he will."

Addie lost her breath. Her whole body tensed as Spencer leveled the knife over her again. He looked like he was thinking, considering. She started to shake her head, to beg. He yanked the chair off her and slammed down hard, his knee landing on her chest, squeezing out what little air was left. She saw the knife raised, leveled over her throat. She couldn't look, wouldn't witness her own demise. She dug her fingers into the floor, crawling, trying to inch away.

And then she felt it.

The pepper grinder.

The knife caught Addie's forearm as she jammed the grinder into Spencer's eye. She felt the cool slice of blade against flesh, felt the drops of her own blood as it bubbled and pooled. But Spencer dropped the knife. He rolled up on to his knees and Addie kicked out, catching him where she didn't know—she didn't stay to find out. She was on her feet while he was hunched, hands pressed to his eye. He was grunting, breathing sharply, letting out a guttural moan that set Addie's teeth on edge.

She ran.

She vaulted across the kitchen and yanked the door to the garage open, slamming her bloodstained fingers against the garage door opener.

Her fingers slid.

Spencer was at the door.

Addie kept running, pulling open the door to the vintage Mustang that her father had bought and that Addie had studiously avoided until that moment. She vaulted herself in, slammed the door lock down just as Spencer reached her, an ugly mask of hate and rage on his face. His left eye was red, bulging and bleeding tears. His fisted hands slammed against the driver's side window.

Addie was shaking, teeth chattering, a weight on her bladder.

Her heart thundered in her chest, the lump in her throat almost choking her.

"Keys, keys." She fumbled, trying her best to block out Spencer clawing at her on the other side of the glass. He was still pounding, his screams muffled, his face distorted by the streaks of blood on the glass.

The keys were in the visor.

As Addie fed them into the ignition, her brain slammed with memories, with anxiety and terror.

She had to drive.

She had to try.

"Gas…uh, parking brake." Her lips felt chapped and raw. The heat inside of the car was stifling, choking—and Spencer was punching, his knuckles blood red and cut.

Addie turned the key.

The engine sputtered and purred.

She yanked the gearshift and felt for the gas pedal with her foot, hands tight on the wheel.

Spencer punched.

The driver's side window buckled, a spiderweb of cracks on the glass. Addie dove to get away from Spencer, steering wheel in hand.

The wheels screeched.

The car lurched.

She heard the sickening thud of body against metal but barely had time to register it. The car vaulted backward though the garage door, crashing in a brilliant burst of twisted metal, buckled wood, and dust.

FORTY-FIVE

Addie was crying, her whole body shaking, the car coming to a rest in the middle of the street as her foot slid off the gas and she collapsed over the steering wheel. She could barely make out anything through the flood of tears, through the buckled, bloodied glass. But she could see Spencer on the garage floor, his body bent, crumpled.

He wasn't moving.

"Addie! Addie! Oh my God, Addie, what happened?" Colton dashed in front of the car, yanked on the driver's side door. Addie froze, hands still locked on the steering wheel, teeth chattering, tears falling.

"Addie!" Colton ran to the passenger side, wrenched open the door.

She blinked at him. "Colton?"

His eyes were soft, brows knitted in concern. "Are you okay? What happened?"

She slowly turned to look out the driver's side window, the dripping blood turning her stomach, the image of Spencer in the background haunting. "I…Spencer, he…" She erupted in a fit of sobs, her shoulders shaking, her chest aching with the effort. She hiccupped and sputtered, snot and tears running down her cheeks.

"Spencer was trying to kill me. He was trying to kill me and I...I think I...I hit him with my car." She yanked her hands off the wheel like it was a poisonous snake, staring incredulously at the dash. "I don't know what I'm doing, I don't know what I did."

Colton stared straight ahead, swallowing slowly. "You hit Spencer with your car?"

"He was trying to kill me, Colton. We have to get out. We have to call the police. I think he killed Lydia, too—I think he's crazy. Colton, come on."

Colton shook his head, carefully, slowly. "You hit him with your car?"

Addie had her hand on the door handle, was trying to force the thing open when she head Colton's low, maniacal laugh. Something cold and dark slithered down her spine, settled in her gut.

"Colton?"

"I'm sorry," he said, hand clamped over his eyes. "I'm sorry but that's just...it's just so funny, isn't it?"

Addie gaped. "What are you talking about?"

He wiped a tear from his eye. "He was supposed to kill you. He was supposed to kill you because your dad bankrupted him and fucked up his family's life. Sorry..." He pat a hand on Addie's shoulder. "It wasn't really about you, it was more about your dad, but, dude, you don't even drive and you hit him with your car."

Addie knew she should get out of the car but she was riveted, horrified, eyes glued to Colton, whose skinny shoulders shook as he giggled. "Man. This wasn't part of the story but"—he shook his head—"I really couldn't have written it better myself."

"What are you—?"

The laughter stopped and Colton's eyes flashed. There was still humor in them, but it was nothing short of psychotic. "I'm the writer, Addie. You write fan fiction." He licked his lips. "I've decided to write true crime."

Addie's whole body seized up, heat burning the back of her neck.

"Wh…what are you talking about?"

"I'm talking about a great story, Addie. I'm talking about a great crime—really, with all the details that really make a book sing, you know? And you, you were my hero."

Addie swallowed, her saliva going down like broken glass.

"It was a lot easier than I thought, really. Talk to Spencer a little bit, turn the screws. You know the reasons people kill, Addie? Oh, you probably do."

Addie ground her teeth, her jaws aching. She cut her eyes away from Colton to the keys dangling from the ignition. Colton did too and snatched them out, tossed them out the open passenger side door.

Addie sprung.

She threw her weight against the driver's side door hoping to hit the handle, and it lurched open, scraping against the street. She landed on her hands and knees, chest and chin scraping the ground, ripping at her jeans and palms, but she didn't care.

She was running.

Addie sprinted back to her house, yanking open the door,

clawing for the phone. Colton was so close she could hear his breathing, hear his heavy footfalls. He threw his arms around her waist, grabbing her in a bear hug. Addie went down hard, Colton on top of her.

"This isn't how it was supposed to go!" he seethed, rage turning his face a deep, blotchy red.

"Tell me then, Colton, tell me how it's supposed to go."

Colton pressed his knee to the back of Addie's neck. She scrunched her eyes shut, letting the tears flow over her nose and onto the marble floor.

She just needed time.

"You read the story," he hissed into his ear, hot breath singing her cheeks. "Crystal was drowned, just like our little Lydia."

Addie's whole body seized up. Lydia's limp form flashed in front of her eyes, the way her arms hung, her body a broken carcass, the life snuffed out.

"You?"

"You said it yourself. Authors need to research." Colton was lording over her, keeping her pinned, his voice a terrible, writhing hiss. "I needed to know how it felt. How it really felt when a soul left a body. And you know what?"

Addie shook her head, afraid to open her mouth.

"It was bliss." He drew out the word and ice water flooded Addie's veins. His lip quirked downward. "Then I ran into Spencer." He shook his head. "So much rage in one little person, you know."

"Because you killed his girlfriend?"

Colton snorted. "No! He was knocking her around anyway.

Kind of a fun little circle. Spencer got flaming mad, and whacked her a time or two. She came to sweet, harmless ole me, cried on my shoulder. Earned my trust." He batted his eyelashes. "I did him a big favor. She was always threatening to tell."

"You're sick. You're as sick as Spencer. And you tried to move in on his girl. And then you killed her."

He rolled his eyes. "Spencer didn't care about it at all."

"About *her*. She was a person."

"He dug it, though. He kind of got obsessed. It was his idea to drop her in the journalism room. The idiot had some good ideas. But you were the one he really wanted. You were his prize. And I was, of course, willing to help. I loved watching you squirm. I hacked into your computer and sent you all those messages. I even put up those pictures just to mess with you. Genius locking you out of your own site."

"Why me?" Addie squeaked.

"Why not? But he underestimated you. We both did. Brava, Addie. You almost got to live. But in the Gap Lake books, Crystal had to die…"

Addie gritted her teeth, digging her fingers into the grout between the tiles and kicking out hard. She felt her foot make contact, heard the clack of Colton's head flipping back, his teeth smacking together.

"But Jordan survives." Addie crawled onto all fours, then was up on her feet, panting, heaving, phone in her hand. "The end."

FORTY-SIX

Addie was laying in her bed propped up with pillows and painkillers while Maya lay at the edge of the bed, flipping through her phone.

"You doing okay?"

Addie tried to shrug, but she was bandaged from fingertip to neck so she offered a pained smile instead. "For almost being killed, yeah."

"Spencer is out of the hospital. He and Colton are being arraigned tomorrow. Murder for what they did to Lydia, attempted murder for what they did to you, battery for feeding poor Louisa rat poison and for trying to make me into a hood ornament. And of a crap car no less." Maya shuddered then blinked, her eyes going glossy.

"Are you crying?"

"I can't be a little emotional that two maniacs tried to kill my best friend?"

"So much for your psychic powers. Could have saved us all a lot of trouble."

"Hey, I'm a sham and even so, who could have predicted that

two kids would read a couple of books and terrorize their next-door neighbor?"

"Okay, who wants raspberry cheesecake and who wants the salted caramel?" Morton Gaines held up two pints of ice cream and a couple of spoons.

Addie handed Maya the raspberry and dug into the salted caramel.

"You know," Maya said, around a mouthful of ice cream. "It's kind of nice having you around to wait on us."

"Well, get used to it," Addie's father said, "because I'm home for a while."

Addie's eyes flashed. "Really?"

"I'm taking a sabbatical." He sat down next to Addie, throwing his legs up on the bed and crossing them at the ankle. "I thought I'd take some time to hang out and really get to know my daughter."

"Maybe teach her how to drive her car forward?" Maya said.

"Maybe spend some time reading," he said, pulling a Gap Lake mystery from Addie's nightstand.

Addie snatched the book from him, dropping it into the trash can with a loud thud.

"No," she said, between bites of ice cream. "I'm done with mysteries for a while."

ACKNOWLEDGMENTS

There are many working parts to writing—and choreographing—a novel and *Copycat* is no exception. I'd like to give my deepest thanks to Steaphen Fick of the Davenriche School of European Arts for dropping a chair on me and helping me choreograph my fight scenes, match weapons to characters, and for teaching me to take out a horde of angry zombies with a garden hoe.

To the LeBoule crew: Julie Carver, Christina Britton, Deb McNaught, Victoria Phelps, and Rich Amooi. You have been my biggest cheerleaders when it comes to writing, but you were even bigger and cheerier when I was diagnosed with breast cancer just before this book was complete. Thank you for the meals, hand-holding, hugs when I got out of the house, and ridiculously long text strings.

Also, a huge debt of gratitude to my summer students at the San Jose Writing Project's Teen Writers Institute. You guys are inspiring, talented, and great at making sure I kept it real while writing and keeping me on my ever-loving toes. And thank you to Kate Flowers and Jeff House for bringing me the best victims—I mean students—every summer!

ABOUT THE AUTHOR

Hannah Jayne decided to be an author in the second grade. She couldn't spell and had terrible ideas but kept at it, and many (many) years—and nearly twenty books—later, she gets to live her dream and mainly does it in her pajamas.

She lives with her rock-star husband and baby daughter and their three overweight cats in the San Francisco Bay area. She is always on the lookout for a juicy mystery, an exciting story, or a great adventure.

FIREreads

 #getbooklit

Your hub for the hottest in young adult books!

Visit us online and sign up for our
newsletter at FIREreads.com

 @sourcebooksfire

sourcebooksfire

 firereads.tumblr.com